The Enemy Within

Acknowledgements

I dedicate this book to the following:

My mother Deloris Alvarez, for her lessons in poise, intellect and strength.

My sisters, Sandra St John and Candyce Williams, who were with me in the hardest of times and continue to support me, despite my inherent arrogance.

Sarah Brayan, whose editing services continue to be paramount in my creative process.

Thanks to all

Joseph Williams

The Enemy Within

Preface

History has taught all of us about war. The Civil wars carnage between brother and cousin, certainly wasn't civil. With the Government censored media, we are deceived into believing new, easier to swallow, terms for bloodshed:

Theatre of Operations, conflicts, and as of late, War on Terrorism.

These deliberate, and I might add, successful attempts in downplaying bloodshed for profit, or whatever the case, can only be regarded as murder.

Over the years, I have spoken to quite a number of Viet Nam Veterans and found that no one would speak of killing, but all would speak of atrocities of war and the effects of returning home to America with the guilt of senseless murder and the Orange Agent sickness that the VA would not treat, because the Government would not acknowledge the its existence for over 20 years.

Their stores inspired this fictional account of death and the sorrows of Government programs gone awry.

God Bless America!

The Enemy Within

Collateral Damage

Saigon 0200 at 200 feet and no sleep for the last 18 hours, due to post Black Op briefing. As the Huey chopper buzzed the tree tops, I surveyed my rag tag crew of the Navy's best. "What Best" I thought, as I dreaded over the sad reality that this battle weary bunch wasn't my own unit or even my choice of men. Recent Viet Cong, (V.C.) skirmishes left my unit pretty thin. This new Op left no time for battle wounds to heal or even debate. West Point drilled into us that "A good soldier always obeys orders". Blind faith you might say. Well, yes, I do obey orders, but I don't have to like 'em. Let's see, what do we have here? Six of Sing Sing's worst. When Nixon uses inmate incentive programs to win the war, one can only assume it's a suicide, one way mission.

Jackson was from Florida and spend his young years as a Ghetto jack boy. With no parents, he grew up on the streets. What he desired, he stole or robbed without conscience.

Jeb Lynch hailed from Georgia and brought four terms of service and a world of experience to the team. A natural woodsman and an even better killer. This "machines" exploits were legendary. The machine reference was due to his cold thin blue eyes that squinted when he relished in the torture and dismemberment of his victims; oops, I mean prisoners. One can only wonder and fear what he did in those Georgia back woods.

Jason Wentworth was a privileged "upper crust" from Boston with immaculate nails and pressed uniform. I can only wonder if he polishes his ammo, spit shine boots in the bush? Bullshit! The shine alone would give up on our position.

"Soldier", I yell.

"Sir, yes Sir, he replied.

The Enemy Within

"Kill that shine, you fancy pants mother fucker, before I show you the fast way to glorious Mother Earth". As you can guess, Wentworth had polish and used it, only not to buff it out, feeling relieved that this blue blood wouldn't cause any of us to lose any of ours, I went on.

Rainsburg was selling ham sandwiches at 200 feet.

"Rainsburg", I said, what the fuck are you doing on Uncle Sam's chopper"?

"I'm getting paid Sir" he replied.

Weapons specialist aside, "stow that shit", was all I could say.

Our medic was Hal Goodbody, a thin model type that made you wonder why he would be in prison in the first place. Well spoken, he only did so when spoken to. Eyes of steel, I felt nervous in his gaze. Those eyes looked through you. I had seen this stare before, and it was always the look of a psychopath. Medical degree or not, I feared the worst with this nut case.

Seebers was our communications operator. We called him Radio Shack, because he could fix anything electrical. At 300 pounds, this giant 6' 5" man was afraid of his own shadow. A winer he was, wa! wa! wa! was all I could hear above the helicopter blades.

"Seebers" I yelled.

"Sir, yes Sir", he answered.

"Shut the fuck up, before I put you out of your fat fucking misery".

"Sir, yes Sir".

Lastly, there was me, Sgt, J. Williams, a poor slob that got caught up in Florida's drug trade with his wife, only to take the weight and lose everything, even her. What could go wrong? Everything! This we knew, but readily accepted, due to an alternative fate; life in prison.

The Enemy Within

All of us were with prior military experience, so I was glad Uncle Sam did its research. The mission was to fly below radar from South East Saigon to the Mekong Delta's 69th parallel, where a POW camp held the commander of VC operations. A fortified camp, this will be a hard target to kill. We were told this operation could possibly end the war, outside of nuking the whole damn place. So why not? As these thoughts ran through my mind, a loud thud and snap rang out into the night. The Huey clipped a tree and we lost our rear rotor. Why? My eyes opened in sheer horror as I see Rainsburg up front with ham sandwiches. Pilot and asshole eating while we plummet to the earth....

Pilot Hobbs was CIA and should have known better, but his flight load, hunger, and that fuckin Rainsburg, I guess, got him in his state of OP combat fatigue.

"Hobbs, Hobbs; damage control, damage control", I yelled.

"Losing hydraulic fluid and losing control". "Sir, can't maintain altitude for long".

"Brace for impact", I yell.

Seebers jumps up crying and runs to the hatch screaming:

"Were all going to die". "I'm getting out of here".

I yell, "Medic secure that hatch and that asshole".

Goodbody runs to the rear and kisses Seebers head with his AK-47.

"AK-47"? I yell. "Where'd you get that"?

Coldly, Goodbody says "I just got it Sir".

"Brace for impact" I yell; just as a loud crack, then lights out.

The warm sun of daylight and smell of gasoline brought me to. Looking around to ascertain damage and our position, I was glad to see no casualties. Our radio, however was DOA. Radio Shack was no help and certainly not a miracle worker. As I figured from briefing maps, we were 20 miles from our target with no turning back, because soon this area would be crawling with the enemy.

The Enemy Within

"Were all going to die"? Oh, no, Seebers again, just as the first patrol passed. We covered the chopper.

"Medic! Medic!" "Quiet that soldier", I yelled, hoping not to be heard.

Goodbody took to the problem at hand, and soon Seebers was once again asleep. Telling Jackson to carry that cry baby; we humped it out of there pronto.

Getting over the hurdle of detection, we pushed on to the first village. Getting food and provisions, we rested and gathered ourselves; that is until Seebers came to, mumbling out loud; I said

"What's the matter, you fat bastard, and cat got your tongue"?

When he opened his blood-filled mouth, he was missing his tongue. Reeling from shock, I say to Goodbody,

"Where the fuck is his tongue"? His reply is "You said to silence him, and I did".

"You'll be court marshalled for this, you asshole!"

"Yes Sir" He smiled.

Looking at Lynch, my #1 man, he only said

"We better be moving out now Sir". "It'll be getting hot with the Cong soon".

All are present, but Jackson and Wentworth. Following the slight whimpers, we find Jackson and Wentworth raping a local girl of about 15.

"Is this your deal, you SOB's"? I say as the child runs out.

"Do you know who she'll bring back"?

Jackson runs out and it's behind us for now; that is until Rainsburg on point, sees a dollar on the side of the road. Oh, no!

"Don't touch that"! BOOM; booby trap.

RIP Rainsburg; that hoppin molly mine did its job and damn near cut his midsection in half.

"Bag him and give me his tags", I say to Goodbody.

The Enemy Within

As Rainsburg lies bleeding to death, he looks down and sees his body torn in half.

"Oh fuck, I am a goner and these bastards are going to bag and tag me, before I can even take my last breath". "Not this way, not like this"!

As Goodbody hovers over him, he whispers

"Medic, please give me morphine, help me please; don't let me die like this"!

Goodbody removes his dog tags and then places the body bag next to him and to Rainsburg's horror, Goodbody rolls the lower half of his torso into the bag. Then he starts to roll his top torso, with chilling indifference, directing his cold black eyes into Rainsburgs, he said

"We need all the morphine we can save and besides, you are already dead".

Rainsburg did not know where it came from in his mangled guts, but he projectile vomited with a vengeance into Goodbody's face. Rolling Rainsburg into the body bag, face up, Goodbody never even blinked or changed his expression. Using his hand to wipe his face, he licks his hand as the chunks of blood, guts and foul smelling bile drips down his chin, like a meatloaf gravy.

"So good, so good", Goodbody says as he looks around to make sure no one was watching. Reaching into Rainsburg's upper body, he pulls out a chunk of liver and looks coldly into Rainsurg's eyes as he nibbles on the warm organ.

Coughing blood, Rainsburg whimpers "Oh Jesus, please help me, please end this misery".

Finishing the last of his treat, Goodbody looks into Rainsburg's eyes and says "You're Jewish, aren't you"?

Rainsburg, breathing a sigh of relief, says "Yes, yes I am. Are you going to give me a proper Jewish burial"?

The Enemy Within

Goodbody turns and moves closer, "Why no, my good man, I just wanted to make sure I was eating Kosher for the next few days. That's how long you'll last, you know. Today for lunch I'll have liver pate and for dinner, I think I will have some kosher sausage".

"Sausage"! Rainsburg tries to yell out. "You fuckin monster"! Feeling his guts churning again, he says "Oh no" and turns his head to throw up. Without expression, Goodbody seized the moment and grabs Rainsburg's hair and yanks his head toward his. Quickly lowering his mouth to Rainsburgs, he chugs down the dying man's innards. Rainsburg could only stare into the Medic's cold eyes is disbelief, after his guts stopped pumping vomit, as he felt him begin to suck for more. How could this be? He thought, as the hollow sound of sucking came from his severed stomach. What is he doing? He thought as Goodbody began to suck on his mouth even harder. At that moment, the Medic's tongue entered Rainsburg's mouth and came into contact with his own tongue. Rainsburg could only pray as he knew what would come next. Goodbody bit down hard on the terrified dying man's tongue. With one bite it left his mouth and was now being slowly chewed and savored. Yes, yes. Yes, the tongue less soldier thought as he felt the all too familiar systems of passing out flow over him. No pain, no reality and no fucking freak to slowly eat you!

Goodbody says "We'll dine later" as he zips up the body bag and the very large Jackson throws it over his shoulders. Rainsburg, waiting for either unconscious darkness or the white light and sweet kiss of death to come upon him. All that came was the semi-conscious state of shock and the bump, bump, bump, as the large young soldier's stride bumped him around on his shoulders. What a way to die, Rainsburg thought, through the searing pain of his final moments. Unable to scream, he felt like a fly caught in a spider's web, slowly being devoured alive.

Pressing on with Lynch on point and Jackson bringing up the rear, darkness falls and we find a place to camp out with Jackson on first watch. With this, I know the shit will now surely hit the fan.

"My Mama and Daddy told me to do this shit, and now my baby Mama won't have a man".

"Hey Asshole", I hear Lynch say, "Children say Mama and Daddy, you're a grown man talking like a fuckin idiot".

The Enemy Within

"Fuck you Cracker", Jackson replies, as Lynch only smiles through squinted eyes.

"Have a light" Lynch says and lights a cigarette.

"Stow that smoke" I say "and don't forget, 3 men on a match". "You want the whole jungle to see us go to sleep"? "Jackson on 1st watch".

We slept soundly, but I still have this gut feeling. About 0400, Jackson, Lynch, and Wentworth sat about, talking when Jackson says

"Hey, what's 3 on a match"?

Lynch smiles and said "Oh, just a silly superstition; want a smoke"? "Sure"

Jackson replies, "Hey man, I didn't mean to call you cracker and are there snipers out here"? "Sure you did, and yes there are". Lynch replied as he lit the smoke, took a drag and passed it to Wentworth.

Jackson sits and quietly whimpers to himself, discerning what his life has become. Is this how I'm going to check out? He thought. Things were safer in prison, he reasoned. After all, three hot's and a cot, wouldn't kill you. At least, not like this! As he pondered the many horrific adventures he encountered as "not like this", he remembered coming to prison as an 18 year old innocent. He figured if he ratted out all of his friends, he would get off the hook. With over thirty charges from drug sales to breaking and entering, there was not getting off. Those fuckin cops lied to me, he thought, as the sentencing judge listened to witness, after witness testify against him:

A Mrs. Sharron Moses, the 81 year old from his neighborhood told how he and three other kids broke into her back sliding door in the wee hours of the night to rob her. As tears welled up in her eyes, she continued her story. After nursing her husband for over ten years, she spoke of feeling helpless as the cancer proved to be stronger than the both of them. The Doctors encouraged continued treatment, which naturally drained all of their funds. The bitch was really pouring it on thick, he thought. Now, she was balling her eyes out, telling how she got a reverse mortgage on their house, to only lose it to a real estate developer. Then, not being able to sleep in her single room for years after the funeral of her dear husband, she heard the glass break. Frozen in fear, she saw the dark figures enter her room.

The Enemy Within

Just then, the defense attorney objected and said.

"Can she identify the perpetrators"?

Without hesitation, she points directly at Jackson and screams

"That's the one, that's the one who hurt me"!

The defense attorney yells back and says

"Madam, were the lights not on and wasn't it dark in your room by your own admission"?

At that point Jackson could take no more of this bitches shit. Jumping up, he raised his shackled hands at her and did some of his own yelling.

"Yeah Bitch, I object too, how could you see me? It was dark and I had a mask on and even disguised my voice. So tell me your Honors, how could this Ho know it was me that hit that tight ass"?

At this point, the Courtroom erupts into a loud chaotic scene of frenzy. One woman clutched her pearls and let out a gut wrenching gasp, seconds before she did a header and hit the floor in a drama filled faint. Jackson's family members stood and yelled, cursed and called him a stupid idiot. With the courtroom now in a complete state of panic, Jackson couldn't and wouldn't understand why? His Lawyer and everyone else was screaming at him.

Now, through all the commotion, there was a new loud noise. Bam, bam, bam went the Judges gavel on the desk. Over and over the judge screamed

"Order, order, order"

Oddly enough, this scene seemed comical to Jackson. The bearded skinny Judge looked like he was a grubby construction worker, hammering some wood.

With order restored, objections overruled and Jackson warned by his Lawyer

"Not to open his stupid pie-hole again"

The Enemy Within

The poor widow continued her testimony against him and his friends. She said that while the others riffled through her limited belongings, the 6 foot, 5 inch Jackson just stood at her bedside with that look in his eyes. She described in horror that something else was in the room. Looking down, she saw his hand holding it, mmmm, mmmm, is what he was saying, as he approached with his "flesh" weapon

"Oh no, oh no, she told of her screams as he told her to

"Shut the fuck up and get some of this good wood".

Covering her mouth with one hand, he used his other hand to place his massive weapon on her.

"Don't worry about your Granny draws", he said, as his member blasted his way through her panties. Unable to scream, she decided she needed air, because this large boy also had massively large hands, that were about to suffocate her. You could hear a pin drop, as she told how on his way into her, he let out a large moan and an even larger wet load into her. Once again, the tears flowed as she told of how in the next 5 minutes, he, like an animal let out another 6 moans and matching loads.

"Oh my God" she yelled out. "He was going to kill me with that thing"!

At that point, another woman hits the floor in a heap.

"Objection"! Yells the defense "What was she doing counting his orgasms"?

Jackson once again jumps up and yells above the crowd. "That ho is lying, because I only busted 3 nuts in that bitch"!

As the other prisoners in the room laughed at him, Jackson was cited for contempt and led away to a single holding cell.

"Fuck all y'all", he yelled, as he was led out of the Courtroom.

"These bitches just don't know", he mumbled, as he looks into the garbage can to gram some discarded lunch. A man has to eat, he thinks, as he finds some half eaten peanut butter and banana sandwiches. Filling his belly, he says. "A man's got to sleep". Seconds later, he drifts into better times, when he was back home.

The Enemy Within

His mind free of the confines of incarceration, it takes him to the pass-times he liked best. At 6 years old, he had the body of an 18 year old, 140lb man. On the school yard, he would hold the girls down and touch them, until the authorities found a more appropriate place for, as they called it "his kind". His kind, he thought, as he wondered how many witnesses were going to tell their sob stories. His mind wasn't the only thing that was wondering, because now his hand wandered into his pants and was now wondering about his member. Soon enough, he was out of control with himself, eyes closed and his fist closed around his throbbing shaft. Yeah, yeah, yeah, he moaned, as he felt his boiling juices start to well up from his oversized balls.

"Hey, what the fuck are you doing inmate"? He heard the guard scream.

"Oh no, oh no, I can't stop it Sir", Jackson yelled out as he jumped to his feet. The guard flings the door open and raises his club to beat Jackson, but unable to control his passion, his member starts its own assault.

"Oh Shit", Jackson says, as he starts to squirt his man fluid like a garden hose.

Caught off guard by the sperm bath, the guard could only retreat for back up. All of this was witnessed in the control room, via closed circuit security cameras that covered every square inch of the Courthouse.

Now alone and unaware of anything else but the wave after wave of pleasure between his legs, Jacksons hand, by instinct, grabbed his rod and threw his head back, closed his eyes and rides it out.

As Jackson stood in front of the camera, feverishly jerking his hand in fast motion, the control room officers watched the monitor of Jackson in shock. The rookie cop straps on his riot gear, not taking his eyes off the monitor and asks

"What's wrong with him Sir"?

The Sergeant turns to him and answers

"That crack baby is the Jacksonville rapist. Old or young, this piece of shit will never see his fuckin hood again".

The Enemy Within

With a puzzled look on his face, the rookie says

"Sir, we only have him on a few counts of rape, and the assault and burglary charges I hear won't stick".

The Sergeants face turns red with anger, as he grabs the rookie's bulletproof vest and screams

"What! Do you feel sympathy for this new breed of black bastard"? "They don't work, they steal everything they want and when they go through their rights of passage by coming to jail, it's a fuckin party with their family and friends". "Twenty years ago, we didn't have to lock our doors and now my dear old Mother can't even go to the market alone". "Alone"!

Shaking the rookie, the Sergeant yells,

"Well, tell me, punk, does your mother walk alone"?

Not understanding why the Sergeant was so worked up, he heard himself answer,

"She has a car Sir; she drives".

The Sergeant freezes delirious with rage, he yells "Move out men". The control room door burst open and the stream of officers looked like choreographed gladiators marching to war. The modern day gladiators had helmets of steel and bulletproof Teflon. Their footgear wasn't leather sandals, but lead weighted steel toed boots. And their swords were batons with a 50,000 volt shock that could take down the largest of men. Lastly, for extra protection for them, of course 100,000 volt shields were deployed because of Jackson's immense physical body and the obvious limited mental capacity.

"Hup, hup, hup, the guards chanted, as they marched down the winding hallways towards the corner. Now in complete silence, in spite of their body armor, lead boots, and gloves they came face to face with an obviously dazed and not finished jerking off Jackson. The rookie whispers "Sarg, he's still at it".

Before the Sergeant can answer, a female lieutenant giggles over the two way radio and says, "He's still at it alright, this boys amazing with his round three".

The Enemy Within

The men heard the female officers in the command center giggling, when the Sergeant yelled out, "Radio silence", "move in; move in".

Jackson, in the throws' of passion didn't even hear the voices. Slap, slap, slap, went his hand on his member and sprayed it just as the guards entered the cell. Crackle and pop was the sound the cops electrified weapons made as Jackson's eyes opened wide.

"Oh no, oh no, someone please help me, please help me"!

The Sergeant led the assault by screaming

"I'll kill you, you son of a bitch".

With any other man, one baton to the gut would have downed him, but not only didn't the man-child go down, but the voltage only seemed to intensify his orgasm. Curling up in the fetal positon, he could only reason to ride out the beating of the cops and his beating meat.

Having passed out, Jackson comes to in the Court holding cell again and realizes he had been out for days.

"Wake up scumbag freak", the rookie calls out to him. "Get ready for court and if you start that freak shit up again, the Sarg said to shackle you". "So if you want to piss and shit on yourself without wiping, go ahead, you son of a bitch".

With a splitting headache, Jackson's first reaction was to say the arbitrary "fuck you", but he held it in for a later day. I'm going to kill this cracker, he thought and smiled.

In and out of jail for years, Jackson knew this punk was a green rookie and like on the streets, he somehow knew he had to kill whoever pissed him off.

Entering the Courtroom, Jackson immediately eyeballed the witness area. Oh no, he thought as he spotted his 14 hear old cousin, crying with her head lowered to avoid looking at him. Just then, his eyes opened in horror as he noticed the large bump that now replaced her once lean stomach.

The Enemy Within

Turning to the general seating area, he looks at the angered glares of family members. Without thought, he yells out.

"I didn't do that shit, hell Nah, that wasn't me; I pulled out before I busted a nut". "Cousin Kesha, tell 'em I didn't nut in you, only your mouth." "Tell 'em Cuz.". "Don't jam me up gal".

Bang, bang, bang, went the familiar gavel and Jacksons lawyer is now yelling to

"Shut the hell up, you retarded bastard"!

The Judge demanding order and the family erupts into loud cursing directed at Jackson. What's the matter? He thought.

With order restored, the proceedings were now in progress. The young girl told of how Jackson at her age of 11, showed her how to touch him, until, as he called it, the milk would come out. She went on to tell how he said that, "since it was milk, it was also good to drink". This went on for years until he told her that at 13 "that itch between her legs could be scratched with his member". Soon enough he was scratching her itch and this baby was the result of his scratching.

Now, lowering his own head, Jackson could only wait as is cousin testified in detail of the years of his sexual abuse. Thinking that things could get no worse, he watched as his girlfriend Tamika, takes the stand. With mouth agape, eyes bulging, and a cold fear rising from his stomach, Jackson now listened as his own girlfriend testified against him.

She told of the robberies, rapes and then to his surprise, murder! Looking at the courtroom officers, he can see the smiles on their faces, as everyone else stared at him with shock and disgust. She told in graphic detail how he liked to beat his victims before he would violently rape them. She said the beatings were short due to Jackson's massive size, but the rapes went on for hours. The younger the girl was, she said, the more pleasure he got out of it. She said Jackson would "get off" if he could "bust a ho out".

The Enemy Within

Silence fell upon the Courtroom as the prosecution asked her just what did she mean by him "busting the girls out".

"You know, she said, splitting them open, breaking apart their koochies". The prosecutor takes a pause to let her statement sink in and repulse the all-white jury even further, then says.

"And you miss Tamika, were you also privy to his brutality"?

Turning to the Judge, Tamika asks

"Your honor, what the fuck did he just say to me"?

Shaking his head, could only direct the prosecution to rephrase his question to the witness.

"Miss Tamika, what I'd like to know at this time, is were you also raped and busted out, as it were, by the defendant"?

Tamika turns to the attorney and says

"The fuck you say, what the fuck you got going on, mother fucker? Yeah, that bitch busted me out with that tree trunk of his. I'm so big down there, I have to pack my pussy with cotton balls so my dude can feel the sides when he fucks me".

"Objection, objection, your Honor".

Jackson hears his attorney yell, but before the Judge can slam his gavel down, Tamika yells out

"No shit, y'all, my niggas 10 inches of pure dick and thanks to Jackson it's like throwing a hot dog down a hallway. My Koochie is big peoples, big".

The Courtroom erupts into laughter as Jackson lowers his head.

With his thoughts and past behind him, Jackson snaps out of it and looks around.

The Enemy Within

Jackson says "So what's 3 on a match"? Lynch replies:

1st man lights – sniper sees target

2nd man smokes – sniper aims

With that said, Wentworth passes the smoke to Jackson and crack – thud, as Jacksons head explodes.

Lynch turns to Wentworth and says,

"3rd man – sniper fires.

"I guess Mama, Dada, Auntie and all that other goo bullshit will miss you asshole", Lynch says, smiling through cold steel eyes. With the warm sensation of brains all over me and our position exposed, it was time to push on.

"Bag 'em and tag 'em" I tell Goodbody, who I notice always seems to be eating something.

"What the hell are you eating at a time like this"?

"Nothing Sir" Goodbody replies through black eyes that I hated to look at, only now they were even more sinister than usual.

I knew something was wrong. It had to be that gut feeling that made me run to the body bag of Rainsburg. Looking inside, I saw a half-eaten Rainsburg. As the warning bells of horror rang inside of me, I now realized beyond a shadow of a doubt, we were not to return. This bunch of monsters were sentenced to a different form of capital punishment. Not only the enemy, but the enemy within. Sickened by this reality, I stagger to my feet as Hobbs vomits,

"This mission is over", I say, "Fuck West Point, every man for himself, and God for us all".

Now to make it home, God help us!

The Enemy Within

THE WHORE HOUSE

Turning to that Pilot CIA scum Hobbs, I showed him my idea of flight with a right cross that launched his wormy ass a good 10 feet. As I un-holster my Colt 45 sidearm and place it to his head, I say

"Tell me what you know son of a bitch, or I'll kill you".

Lynch speaks up and says

"And just that, you'll have to do Sir; he will die before he talks". "The CIA J. Edger boys train them well".

I reply; "Yeah that fag Hoover knows what he's doing".

Everyone speaks up at once. "Fag Hoover Sir"!

I say "Forget it" and turn to Lynch. "I need this one to talk, and I need you to get it out of him".

"Yes Sir; with pleasure Sir", Lynch replied.

"Wentworth, tie up this scum for transport, I don't want him getting away before I get to the bottom of this shit". I turn to Lynch, "What are our chances of getting out of here"?

"Slim as a group Sir", he replies.

"Should we head for water"? I say.

He said "No, that's where they'll ambush us and I ain't ready to die; I reckon".

 "In that case, I say, let's leave them a calling card, courtesy of Rainsburg".

The Enemy Within

Locating the direction of birds in flight, Lynch gave the direction of the nearest river. In that direction, we set up a booby trap. Another bouncing Betty strung between two trees. When tripped, that thing jumps 4 feet in the air and blows up all flesh at four feet. Mostly legs, dicks and balls. It hardly kills, but once exposed to its treachery, one doesn't have the urge or ability to carry on fighting, dickless; would you?

Goodbody says, "You don't mean it when you said "Every man for himself did you Sir"?

"What are you eating, you maggot". I answer; Nuggets Sir, tastes like chicken", Goodbody says.

Looking closely, I see fingers. You mean digits, you maggot scum; while I proceed to bash his head on the ground.

Lynch breaks us up and says "We're going to need all the firepower we can get Sir".

"OK, I say, but do you feel that Lynch"?

"You mean, us being followed"?

"Yeah", I say. "And how long"?

Lynch replied. "From the start Sir".

"Friend or Foe"?

"Friend", Lynch says. This backwoodsman knew his shit and I never second guessed his judgment. What I did question, was him not being a commissioned officer, and was Lynch his real name? So far, everything out here was a lie.

"Animal or man" I say.

"That depends", Lynch said as he smiled through those slits he called eyes.

"Bring him in alive" I say.

"With pleasure Sir", he responds.

"Alive isn't your pleasure, you freak", I say.

The Enemy Within

"We best be movin on Sir", Lynch says, and smiles.

"Not before we bury our dead; that is, all that fuckin cannibal Goodbody hasn't eaten yet".

Through all of this, I notice Lynch missing, and order quietly to stand down. As we wait in silence for what seems an eternity:

Lynch calls out "Up here Sir".

Looking up, there is Lynch and another watching us.

I say, "How long were you up there".

And he says "No one ever looks up"; an hour Sir".

Then I see him; I don't believe my eyes. As Lynch and the stranger shimmy effortlessly and silently down the tree,

Wentworth says, "Just like monkeys without the slightest effort".

Agreeing, I lost sight of them,

"Where'd they go"? I said.

"Here Sir" Lynch said standing directly behind me.

"How do you do that"? I said, only to have him squint those eyes.

"Meet Davidson, Sir" Lynch said.

Here, this man child stood at 6 feet 10 inches and 350 lbs.; only one thing, he had the strangest baby face and a mind to match. "They call me Preacher, and bless you Sir" Davidson speaks up.

"They should call you Tank, biggen", I say.

The Enemy Within

Hailing from Florida; Davidson actually signed up for the draft when he lost his family. "How", I asked. Through tear-filled eyes that showed emotion, he said he'd talked about "that" later, because they are here. Turning to Lynch that wasn't there yet, again. I ask "Davidson,

Who's here"?

Before he could reply, a flurry of automatic gun fire rang out.

"Head due east for safety Sir", he said. Then he said "And pray".

With that, he handed me a Bible and held his own and walked directly into the gunfire singing. To my surprise, those baby tear-filled eyes were now candy apple red, and dripping blood, even though he was hit midsection. Was this child mad?

"Davidson, Davidson; Preacher "I yell, with tears in my own eyes.

Into the Frey, he went with only a pump Mossburg shotgun, boom Onward Christian Soldiers, marching off to war, boom. To fight the fight of Jesus, boom, boom. Then silence.

"We fought a good fight and that man is a hero" I say.

I feel Lynch behind me and say

"Get his body"

"Won't be any, he replied.

Not to second guess Lynch, we couldn't find Davidson; we did find 20 bodies though. Vanished to where? I thought,

"Better be movin out due east", Lynch said. "We can reach the house by night fall."

"What house" I say.

"The Whore house Davidson told me about", Lynch said.

The Enemy Within

Not getting laid in 10 years, I nor anyone else had a problem with that. Due East, we headed out. "Boom". Oh my, it seems Rainsburg message was delivered.

Placing Lynch on point where I could watch him, that is barring any of his "Houdini" disappearing acts.

"Hey Lynch", I said, "Do you think Davidson made it out OK, or was he taken prisoner"?

"They could never take him alive Sir". "They've been down too long", he replied.

"They"? I ask,

"Yes Sir, there are hundreds of American prisoners out here that probably won't make it home".

"Why", I ask;

"Cuba dumped theirs, and the US is too embarrassed to change the inscription on Lady Liberty". "Who better than prisoners saves a ton of money", he said.

"But were dying, for what"? I ask.

"There's oil here Sir, Mattel INC., the toy company just made a new gun called the M-16 and many other companies like Grumman, Lockheed Martin, and a small start-up funded by the members of congress named Halliburton. All have vested interest in war. As a stock holder in these no-bid approved companies, you would be a rich man, and they are all rich men Sir", he replied.

"What about the locals and American sentiment"? I say.

"With their land invaded and pillaged for its resources, the locals will rise and fight any invader for its sovereignty and its way of life. In return, Government controlled media will deem what its very foundation was based on in 1776's Revolution as evil; Patriots are now terrorists and wars are now "wars on communism". In the future, that will change to terrorism; through selective media coverage, Americans will go anyway; the media tells 'em, like puppets", he said.

The Enemy Within

"Soldier that sounds like pink-o communist propaganda to me", I said.

"It's the world run Zionist Sir".

I hear Davidson say from behind me.

"Davidson where have you been"? I ask.

"The Trees Sir," They don't look up.

"Oh Lord, what's next? I say"

"Hallelujah" Davidson said.

Pressing on till dusk, we reach the "House". This wasn't a house, it was a two-story brick and mortar building. Here's that gut feeling again. Out steps something out of what seems "The Bahamas" with sandals, shorts, Hawaiian shirt and says

"Hi, I'm Kenny, your host at your service. Please come in".

Once inside, like any other run of the mill perfume drenched multi-room house of tramps. We eyed a bevy of women to die for. Tall, short, fat, slim; all Viet Cong. At fat VC? All here were healthy, in spite of the rot gut indigenous, twice a day plate of sun dried fish heads over rice. Concrete and plump VC? That gut feeling again.

"Line up and drop your shorts, Kenny says". This is Ling; she will give you whatever you need".

She went down the line of men and squeezed our dicks, then washed our members;

"Why squeeze". I asked Lynch.

"The clap" was all he said as he took a room with a whore. As everyone paired off, my luck left me in a large room full of mattresses.

The Enemy Within

"What's that smell" I asked Davidson.

"VC Gold Sir, Oh, meet Jackson, or big dummy, as we call him".

"Hey, any relation to you know, the one from Jacksonville"?

"Yes, Sir, cousins, Sir", he said.

Just looking at this 6 food 8 inch beast. I could only guess why they called him Big Dummy.

"Are you a freak, Big Dummy"? I asked.

"No Sir, he replied.

"A man poker"? I ask. "No Sir, he replied.

"Ever have a 9-5 job big dope" I say.

"No Sir, he answered. "Figures", I say.

"Fall out men, I say, then turn to Ling Ling and say
"Come on babe, let's get it on".

Ten years without the touch and only the smell of female guards. I knew this wouldn't take long. I notice Kenny in the shadows staring at us like a mental patient.

"What's this going to cost us", I ask.

Oh, we'll work it out Sir, He said.

"Good, now mind your fucking business you pervert".

"10 years of back stall boom boom room jacking off; I think I deserve a little privacy and

"Hey" are those bones shaved off of your forehead? "Looks like horns"?

With this, he smiles and says "Want a light"?

As he leaves, "What the hell was that" I ask.

The Enemy Within

Ling Ling comes close and is now naked with a large ass and boob job. Boob job in the bush? That gut feeling; 10 years? Who the fuck cares, I'm going to bust my nuts all night long.

"Come on now Blackie, Ling Ling love you long time", she said.

"You got that right, and what's with this Blackie shit? Look what that word did to my dick. "Bitch, you better get to slurping you VC whore".

"Sure Blackie, me make you cum boo coo time", she said as she took every inch of my dick down into her throat.

"Hey, what's this", I ask.

"Deep throat" she says as she worked her head.

Cum throat, I figured at this pace. The girls back home need to learn this.

"Yeah, yeah, yeah, not just the head, every inch". I say as Lynch says from behind me,

"Come Sir".

"If you get the fuck out of here, I'm going to do just that; cum down this whores throat", I said.

Tap, tap, tap! "Come this way Sir, you have to see this shit", he says.

I realize this man won't disappear when I ask him to. So I get to see what's so important to stop a man from getting laid after 10 years. Sure enough, Lynch came through. In the middle of the room was a large mattress and a large naked black ass man, with an 80 pound whore with the biggest tits I've ever seen on a woman. Big Dummy was kissing and licking those big tits; next to him was a plate of sausages!

"What's the food for"? I asked Lynch.

"Protection; cause some of those VC put razors up there, and when soldiers rape them, a shredded dick is their revenge before they die", he said.

"Jesus", I say,

"No, war", Lynch replied.

The Enemy Within

With this, big dumb ass; he takes a sausage, dips it in some k-y jelly and slowly moves a few inches into her waiting wet pussy lips.

"Jesus, can she handle that 12 inch sausage", I ask.

Not noticing big dumb asses package, Lynch says.

"Look what's next Sir". She lifts her head as he blows his first nut down her throat. She swings around and says

"Yes, Blackie, more, yes, Blackie, more; as she lowers herself onto what seemed to be a 16 inch dick. Inch at a time, up and down; a little deeper each time with each squirt;

"Blackie, yes, Blackie, yes" she said as her eyes rolled back in her head. Now as she pumped that idiot horse cock dry, she put those huge tits into his mouth and it was on again.

"Go man, go" I said. "Holy Shit", what a show! Jackson.

Big Dummy jackass, it would seem, was quite the ladies' man. He propped her up doggie style, and slammed his rigid dick up into her to the 16 inch hilt, wham, wham; her hairless pussy could take no more, when once again this pro moves onto his face to give him what she had. He stuck out his tongue and she went up and down on it, while her white cream ran down his mouth and chest. As she screams,

"Oh Blackie, Oh Blackie".

Big Dummy unloads yet again, this time all over her back as she now puts his shooting member to the entrance of her forbidden zone. As the cum lubricated her ass, he slowly slid in just a little. The hot cum now being slowly pumped into her quivering ass made her pussy come alive again; wave after violent wave of pleasure swept through her as her pussy squirted cum down her quivering weakened legs. By this time, Big Dummy was deep stroking that little ass in fast motion; slap, slap; his balls rang out, as he buried his cock home. Yep, you guessed it, Wad #3 came with a loud moan from the Dummy.

The Enemy Within

Starting to cum again in her ass, she pulls him out and tit fucks him using her mouth at the same time. What a hot mess! This idiot wasn't good for anything else in life, but this; and this, he did well. A little too well, cause with cum shooting everywhere; a load hit my pants.

"Son of a bitch" I say, "I can't take this torture anymore".

Feeling Ling Ling tug on me saying,

"Come on Blackie, let's go, let's go".

I say "You call me Blackie, and when this is over, I will call you "guts on the walls".

"What you mean by that Blackie" she says; "Come here and kiss her" I say, as I plan on fucking and cumming all over all of them. Just as I slide my junk into the tightest, hottest wet pussy I ever felt, I feel my load churning up in my balls. Won't last long, I think, as a tap, tap, tap on my shoulder brings me out of my sexcapade.

"Hung sung Ho" someone yells.

"What's that", I yell, "That's a pineapple that goes boom", Lynch says.

"Pineapple" I say; "RPG" Lynch answers as the grenade comes crashing through the window. Everyone grabs a mattress and covers; Dumbass takes his mattress, kicks the girl away and covers. I grab Ling Ling for cover and "Boom!" The RPG goes off.

"All secure"? I yell as Dumbass runs out the door yelling,

"I surrender; I'll tell you whatever you want to know".

"We're OK" Lynch said.

"Where's Kenny" I say through the hail of now, gun fire.

"There" Lynch said as Kenny ran out the door yelling to the Cong;

"I'm on your side, I'm on your side".

"Is there any loyalty around here", I say, turning to Ling Ling.

The Enemy Within

Oops, too bad, Ling Ling didn't make it. Goodbye, guts on the wall.

"Lynch, lay cover fire so we can get the hell out of here". I say.

"No need; Choppers landing on the roof" he said.

"Fall back to the roof", I yell as we file into the chopper.

Safely, lifting off, I think of Ling Ling and her tight pussy, and my still filled balls; I didn't get a chance to empty. My fucking luck, I thought. We'll be headed home soon, I thought, then "Crack, Boom"! The sound of anti-aircraft fire snaps me out of our adventure at the Whore House.

"We're hit" someone yells out, and were going down"!

"Shit! Not again".

The Enemy Within

THE DEMILATARIZED ZONE (DMZ)

"Lynch, Lynch; damage control", I yell, as I see the pilot fall from his chair, wounded by the shrapnel of anti-aircraft fire. CIA scum Hobbs jumps on the controls and says,

"Losing fuel Sir",

"Range"? I ask and he said

"We're over the DMZ, but we can make it to Alpha Charlie rendezvous".

Those words and that gut feeling made me think back 10 years when my friend introduced me to a hick from Georgia that would pay 3 times the money for my drugs. Who but a cop would do such a stupid thing, I thought, as I ignored my gut feeling at the time. Well, he was a cop and nowadays I never ignore that feeling.

"Put her down here, and now". I yell.

"But Sir, we can clear the jungle in enough time to be safe".

"Isn't the DMV "safe", I say, "and so far, I don't like your idea of safety"?

With that, I totally lose it and draw and fire at the control panel.

"Put this bird down now, or I'll put her down my way".

Bang, bang, bang; three more rounds fired into the helicopters flight control panel. Like it or not, this bird was going down, and that she did. "Hard".

Most of Viet Nam, courtesy of the DuPont chemical company was sprayed with a defoliant called Agent Orange. Jungle, homes, men and whatever got in the way, got the orange. A forest could be cleared in a week. Little did we know what it would do to us in 10 years'? No Agent Orange was needed in a non-combat zone, this fact rained true with the retched sound of crashing, twisted metal. Through this hell, Davidson stands up with Bible in hand and says

"Everyone Pray"! Then begins to sing "Onward Christian Soldiers, marching off to war, to fight the fight of Jesus" Oh no, I think, then once again, lights out.

The Enemy Within

Coming too, yet again, I begin to wonder just how much head trauma I can take.

"Lynch report", I say.

"All secure but Hobbs Sir". He says.

"Where is he", I ask.

"There Sir", says Goodbody, pointing to Hobbs, thrown a good 50 feet from the wreckage, impaled through the head on a tree branch.

"Bury him Goodbody", I say.

"Yes Sir", he answers.

"Whole", I say as Goodbody complies. This done, I ask,

"What are we in for now" and Lynch replies.

"We're in too deep Sir, The DMZ is a jungle of death; many renegades, both us and them". "Better be movin out Sir".

"We can find shelter ahead". Davidson says

"I'm not going to even ask how you know this soldier; move out, and Davidson, take point", I say.

Reaching a large hut in a clearing at nightfall, I decide to do recon first. Yeah! What gives here? Sure enough, that Jackson and Kenny were held up there with not a worry in the world or in this case, the jungle.

"I want them dead and I want them quiet". I tell Lynch.

Bunking down for the night, our rations tasted like a steak dinner compared to prison food. As I gobbled down my cold spam in a can, I noticed not a word in the camp site was spoken. The stark realization of a prison pardon to becoming a prisoner of war was sobering to say the least. As for me, I fear no man, but this day fear came to town like an uninvited guest. I knew in my heart of hearts that fear was going to be around a long time. My men looked up to me for assurance and strength and now wasn't the time to show a shadow of weakness.

The Enemy Within

I just survived ten years of prison hell, where murder was commonplace. Only secret and on the sly, because after all it's illegal. Rape was also a daily and nightly routine that will never be stopped. Looking back, I remembered my family and job as an electrical foreman. They say that families never fight on paydays and I have to agree.

Fooling around with another man will likely expose you to the AIDS virus and prison tattoos most certainly brings the slow death of hepatitis C. Unsanitary conditions also brought infections that often resulted in gangrene. Gangrene without antibiotics results in amputation. Even if you were fortunate enough to get out, without most of your limbs, you would be half the man you were when you came into this unfamiliar and inhospitable land.

The only true redeeming pleasure I could get was the hustle and my newly acquired taste for extremely large Southern female guards. Before the prison was built, they were pig and vegetable farmers. Intimate relations at any jobsite ultimately became common knowledge. Not only is that bad for inmate relations, but those pig farmer women have pig farmer brothers and husbands. Taking the risk ultimately results in many beatings. But in life, I figured everyone at one point or another, has to take the beatings.

The beatings didn't stop, neither did I, and soon enough I worked my way up to the Camp Major's wife. Boy they beat me under a table and when they could not reach me anymore, they kicked me. After a brief hospital stay for broken ribs, I guess the Sergeant told her husband that she was in love with me. There were many things she told me about her mundane life. I guess having sex with me in the Officers bathroom, brought her not only happiness and sexual fulfillment, but a temporary escape from an abusive marriage. It would seem that male guards that beat and abuse on the job, also do the same at home.

The Enemy Within

Poor Sarg! All I could do was lavish the loving sentiment on her that she was obviously not getting at home. I knew it couldn't last and with her transfer also came mine. It was the same all over the county, because illicit sex with the female guards happened in every prison. Viet Nam? Why the hell not!

Straight away I learned that the top dogs were the ones with something to sell. It's amazing, but expectations in prison are limited to say the least, but the man with the store, is the man! That's how I survived after I received my sixty year sentence. When the government programs for inmates came about, I like many had no choice but to, you might say, enlist.

So many other prisoners were being shipped to New York City for medical testing at Belleview Hospital's cancer center. To me the only benefit to that option was to die of cancer or worse, the side effects of cancer treatment, in a New York hospital prison ward. At least in a hospital, one could get treatment, unlike the prison system that is in place to make a profit on inmate labor and life. There hospital and medical treatment are almost non-existent. Most men, in addition to natural ailments, will die from AIDS and Hepatitis C.

Seventeen years of sobriety, but suffering multiple injuries left me with many painkillers. Being a sin to flush money, in the form of pills, down the toilet, was out of the question. J.R., the waste of human flesh that he was, used to always beg for a few pills for his aches and pains. After all, we are union brothers. Well, J.R, needed pills and I needed mula. For years, my girlfriend, being a nurse with a drug problem of her own, had full access to prescription drugs. Even though she gave me tons, I traded them for stomach pills that believe it or not, my non-English speaking Indian doctor refused to prescribe for me. So here I am now a small time drug dealer. The bills were not paid, but still my family went to the mall almost every weekend. This behavior couldn't come to any good and sure enough I end up in jail surrounded by the scum of the earth and abandoned by my family.

The Enemy Within

How about the fact that at the time I was not aware of my declining mental state, which didn't permit me to work a full forty hour week, due to a life-long battle with depression. The kind you gradually succumb to, until its sinister grasp has affected every aspect of your life. Little did I know that I was also suffering from Cancer.

Did I address these issues? Nope! I remained in denial, creating a recipe for disaster, if there ever was one. A blind man could have seen through the proposition of the one employee that no one, myself included, trusted. To sell drugs! I will never forget the overwhelming sensation of sheer disgust whenever I came into contact with this piece of shit. I honestly believe that the world would have been a better place, if on the night he was conceived, his father would have fucked that cum dump mother of his, in her rancid ass instead. Wishful thinking, in retrospect, fate and the good Lord brought this devil into my life, to end the mundane charade that masqueraded as my marriage.

So when the end of the month rolled around, my Florida pay didn't cut it. What to do, but sell bootleg tapes. That worked out well until the cops raided the Flea Market I was selling them at. I did not know that Florida was so serious about copy write infringement. Man, they lock you up for that here? I thought. The tip-off came in the nick of time, so when the cop cars filed through the Flea Market entrance gates, I sat low in my car seat as I passed them on my way out. I wonder how much time I would have gotten for some damn movie sales. I thought. Let's see what else I can sell for some extra money. The Pizza game was a great after work job. The only thing was I was delivering Pizza in a Mercedes Benz. Something just wasn't right. Could it be the monthly irresponsible monthly ritual of juggling what bills will and will not get paid. Nope! Was it the shopaholic wife and child's weekly shopping sprees that I enthusiastically condoned? Nope!

The Enemy Within

At sunlight, we storm the hut only to find it empty.   Once again Lynch and Davidson were MIA.   Wentworth and Goodbody were as surprised as I when Jackson, Kenny and a few renegade Cong got the drop on us.

"You assholes will fetch a pretty penny", Kenny says.

"Yeah, and so we won't have to carry you, you'll walk to your graves Jackson says.

Kenny through blackened eyes said, "Only if the jungle doesn't kill them first" then laughs.

"March", he says as we move out.

The hot, not damp, but wet jungle was no joke, as we slowly made our way to a VC secret stronghold. Could this be the location of our original mission? I thought. Where is Lynch and that nut job Davidson when I need them most? Approaching a small hut, Jackson once again decides to show more of his true colors by saying,

"I'm going to rape this gook".

Little did he know, the family knew of our arrival and lay in wait. As we waited outside by the river, I notice a beautiful golden hue come and go.

"What's that, gold fish"? I ask

"Who knows? Not much is known deep in this bush". Wentworth says.

Just then, screaming naked Jackson came running out of the house with a bloody minced Johnson.

"Razor blades" was all we could say, as Jackson ran into the river.

As he soaked his member, the pretty golden mass soon was all around him. Seconds later, he let out a blood chilling yell as the water turned red with his blood.

"I give up, I'll talk, he screams, like a woman.

"You won't talk any more". I say as the pretty fish ate more and more.

"Sir, please, please they'll be here soon with orders from up top to take no prisoners".

The Enemy Within

You said prisoner you maggot scum, that's a bad selection of words. Enough of this bullshit, I say, as I draw, aim, and blow this dumb asses head off.

As he falls into the water, I yell "haul ass" while the fish are feeding.

We jump into the river and as the VC fire, we swim even harder as the golden fish finish up Jackson and now head for us. As they start to nip at our feet, a large object is tossed into the water. The water Buffalo head did its job and distracted the fish long enough for us to reach shore and a waiting Kenny.

"I told you, you'd pay later", he said as he raised a large machete.

"Not this time, Lynch said from above",

"What"? Kenny said as a VC 3 step Viper dropped onto him and sank it's fangs into his chest. Attempting to run, he only made it 3 steps, then fell dead.

"Good to see you Lynch, I knew you and Davidson would get us out of this, and where is he anyway"? I ask.

"The trees Sir, no one looks up". Lynch answers.

"Yeah, yeah, I know", I say.

Goodbody says "Bury our dead Sir"?

"No, there not ours", I answer.

"Feed the fish"? He asked. I don't answer, then he says, and me? All I can say is bon appetite, and hurry up maggot; tap, tap, tap.

"It's time to move out Sir", Lynch says.

"Where to now". I ask, ready to surrender to all this bullshit.

"The camp is dead ahead", he answers.

"Move out", I say, as we head deep into the jungle. Soon enough in the clearing was a well-fortified camp.

"What do you think"? I ask Lynch. He only smiles, then "Boom, boom",

"Everyone pray", Davidson says with blood filled eyes.

The Enemy Within

"Where was he"? Oh, never mind, no one looks up; I know, I answer myself. Davidson walks directly into the camp. Onward Christian Soldiers, "Boom, boom, boom", this went on for an hour, then silence. Upon inspection of the dead, the head of VC operations was also identified. Among the dead, once again wasn't Davidson. Tap, tap, tap on my shoulder, was Lynch.

"Yeah, yeah", I cut in before he could get it out. "Time to move out", I say. By night we traveled not to be detected till we came to a lake.

"We can camp", Lynch said, but don't swim in the blood lake, Davidson says from behind me again.

"I'm not going to ask", I say, as I prepare to go to sleep. "Wentworth, take the first watch".

Morning came too soon with the sound of splashing and frolicking fun. "Wentworth, why did you disobey a direct order". I say.

"Nothing wrong with this lake", he says as he comes out of the water. To our horror, he is covered from neck to feet with banana sized leaches! All at once, they start to feed and not only does he feel it, but starts to shrivel up like a deflated balloon.

"Help me, please", he yells.

"The Lord giveth and the Lord taketh away" "Boom"; Davidson says as he blows Wentworth's head off.

"Sir, meet Kim Ling" Davidson says, as I lay eyes on a mix raced black – VC freckled faced girl of about 20 years old.

"Hey, is Ling Ling your Mom"? I ask with good English, she answers

"Yes, have you seen her"?

"Yeah, she's quite well known and enjoyed, I mean, liked", I say.

Tap, tap, tap, "We better be moving out", Lynch says;

"To my village"? Kim Ling says.

"Why not, move out", I say.

The Enemy Within

Pressing on and talking to Kim Ling for hours, I was growing quite fond of her. Her village came soon enough and I was surprised to find Americans, VC and mixed VC. A lot of them. "Destabilizing the country".

Davidson reads my mind and says, "They need us Sir; their country and ours turned their backs on them and us."

"Is that why you guys stay"? I asked.

Tap, tap, tap. "There here". Lynch said.

"Who is "They" this time"? I ask.

"The Americans", he answered as the chopper lands and all rush to it, but no one enters.

"What's the matter, don't you guys want to go home"? I ask.

Kim Ling stands and cries out,

"Wake up Joe, you have no home, stay with me".

That gut feeling again, I don't know exactly why, but I didn't board that chopper, only Goodbody did, and said,

"See ya suckers" as the big bird lifted off.

"Let us pray", Davidson said and just then "Ka-blam", the chopper exploded.

Sinking to my knees, I cried out

"Oh God, please help us in our time of need".

Davidson says "We can have a wonderful wedding Sir, and you will have beautiful children too".

Marriage, children, I so love the United States, but, oh well, let's see what happens; mission accomplished.

The Enemy Within

KIM LING'S LIE

Our mission was accomplished. The head VC scum was now dead (or in heaven) courtesy of Davidson's shotgun to the face. The double blast took his head clean off! The resulting carnage was nothing short of a bloodbath. Thousands of rounds were fired, but Davidson emerged completely unscathed. This weird shit was going down in this lie of a war. After ten years in prison, they said I was now free. Free? "Yes". In a war-battle combat sense. Freedom, or a license, as we called it to rape, pillage, kill women and bomb laden children. Let us not forget, all the drugs some of us needed to do such acts of atrocity. It was very hard to do, at first. A baby lay crying on the side of the road and when a good-hearted soldier stops to help it, the hidden grenade booby trap trips and kills, or worse yet, maims him to the point of no return. No return to battle, that is. And when he returns home, no return to society, as he once knew it. Now, he is a victim of the Veterans Administration bureaucracy. The quality of post war injuries and hospital care are the direct result of budget cuts, elections and the ever battling congress. As with prison, it is easier and cheaper to amputate a limb than treat it over time. After all, soldiers like an inmate, are expendable. I was an inmate and now as a soldier, I knew this.

These thoughts had run through my mind for months and the ever elusive Davidson didn't make matters any better. With him and Lynch around, we never had casualties. They were good, but no one is that good, of this earth. That hick woodsman and that baby-faced bible thumping man child, made me at ease, but deep down my gut told me something wasn't right. In battle, I saw Davidson get wounded, but later he bore no wounds, nor did Lynch and they never hung around long enough to shed any light on the type of questions that could lead to any possible truths. Kill the goose with the golden egg or shut the hell up and relish every possible living moment we have alive in this hell they call Viet Nam. I may have done the latter with my mouth, but the eyes don't lie, and mine didn't, nor did those squints Lynch called eyes. When that man smiled, hell, we was downright scary.

The Enemy Within

It took a while, but after Davidson performed the wedding, Kim Ling and I lived in what you might call a jungle bliss; a paradise in a VC jungle. How absurd can that be? Is there any bliss in oneself when evil carnage is all around? Hell no, because when people around you are being killed for reasons no one seems to be informed of, it all seems senseless. We were suspicious and unhappy. My love and devotion for Kim Ling paled in comparison to my desire for true freedom and the American way. I'd take my chances in the alleys of Harlem, to the tenements and crack houses of the lower east side, before I could adjust to this jungle shit.

Kim Ling was devoted and a wonderful wife. Her oriental customs dictated subservience. American solders found this trait to be quite attractive and there were no laws to the contrary. I however, had a problem with a woman with opinion less tight lip. Women, the beautiful creatures, they are, cannot keep a secret, but will harbor hate, hurt, and resentment for years or until the occasion arises to exact their revenge. When she tolerates her "stepping stones" toil, for her monetary gain, the end can only result in emotional and financial ruin. This was the case with each of my marriages. Animalistic attraction wanes to cold stares. Wanton sex, all day, every day wanes to accusations of insanity and perversion. These actions were said to be enjoyable in the eve of the relationship, but even the good hot fire of passion can be extinguished by an onslaught of paranoia, fueled by insecurity. My happiness, now fleeting and suspicion driving me mad, I obsess, who is she with? Who will take my place? The answer, as always, was there all the time. It's true that loving eyes shade the truth.

Lynch and Davidson came and went as they wished. The DMZ even neutral as it was, had its danger zones. Snipers, death trees laden with 3 step viper snakes, booby traps, mines and the arbitrary surprises one can think of in a war situation. Lynch did help us as much as he could when he came through, but opted for the fight. I heard whispers of cowardice throughout the camp, but never let it bother us, because we had women after not having any outside of an occasional female officer. Testing the taboo waters of prison sex, these encounters were far in between, but greatly appreciated. Now this newly found freedom and Kim Ling also brought delusion. Kindness and respect go a long way with me and I know not everyone gets along.

The Enemy Within

There was, however, one asshole that no matter how hard I tried to tolerate home, he always put me down in front of Kim Ling. At first, this mutt of a captain got my respect because of his rank, even though rank was nonexistent in the DMZ. I also began to notice his need, excuse or bullshit reason to be around Kim Ling, my wife. Only now did I notice the lack of devotion and Kim Lings tight lip subservience was a past memory.

Day after day Captain Davis berated me to the point of madness. How could I catch this man in the act then kill him, while retaining the respect and loyalty, I so rightly deserved. I thought long and hard and prayed even harder. Then, one night in a dream, the answer came to me. What would Micaville's the prince do? Quite the manipulator and even finer strategist. The princes plan would have to not only eliminate his enemy, but also strengthen his respect and standing in the community. That's right, I thought, as I stirred out of my sleep. Solve all my problems and still come out the hero. Shit, there will go yet another wife. Oh well, and where is she anyway?

Lynch and Davidson just happened to be in camp and I knew even at this ungodly hour of 0300, they would hear me approach and wake up. Keeping my best men near me, my walk to their bamboo hut only took minutes. Not bothering to knock, I entered to find the hut empty. With only one entrance or exit for that matter, I had been through this scene a hundred times before. Without even turning around, I say

"Report to my hut at first light". I don't know from where, but they say

"10-4 Sir".

Returning to my hut, Kim Ling is there and washing up.

"Where were you"? That must have been a hell of a walk for you to have to wash afterwards. It would seem your panties also got soiled enough to wash from "your walk". "Kim Ling, please tell me what's wrong and what's going on".

In desperation, I told her I loved her, only to her response of silence. In the past, as with any couple, an "I love you" prompts and "I love you too". Not this time, however. I also knew that a woman, through guilt, must justify her actions by using anger to do her dirty work. More and more she would pick fights, then disappear for hours.

The Enemy Within

I remember when we would disappear for hours together also. As I come up behind her, I hold her and smell her hair. As I did, the odor of China Gold pot filled my nose. Only one person smoked China Gold and it was Captain Davis. Was my wife now smoking that shit also? Forcing that from my mind, I reach around to her privates only to have her push my hand away and say

"No Joe, not now. Is that all you think of?"

"Well considering I haven't touched you in weeks. Yes, it has crossed my mind, as of late Kim Ling".

"Stop Joe", she said.

"Ok" Then I went to bed. Tomorrow we'll straighten this out. Good night. This bitch is dead, I thought.

The morning daylights sun rays shone through the trees all too soon. I awoke to Kim Ling's absence and Lynch and Davidson's presence. As I look at Lynch, I ask

"Where is Kim Ling"? He smiles through squinted eyes.

"You know where. What you thinking Sir is to murder a commissioned officer"?

"No", I say, let's just have our roast today and see what happens. I'm sure things will work their way out".

"And the Lord will settle the rest", Davidson chimes in.

Just when Kim Ling enters and smelling of pot and sex, she goes straight to the wash basin to clean up. Lynch looks at me, smiles and grits his teeth and says

"It will work out fine Sir". Winks his eye and leaves.

Davidson said "Trust in the Lord" and leaves also.

The Enemy Within

Kim Ling says "What's that all about"?

"Oh, just the cookout. How about some lovin? Are you in the mood?

"Joe, why do you hassle me so"? She said.

"Don't sweat it", I say as I get dressed and round up the men to start the fire for our special occasion.

Today was Christmas and our feast consisted of slow roasted water buffalo. This meat is just like beef, only larger. Potatoes and fish with Kimchi; a cabbage that is buried until fermented rotten. As gross as that may sound, this delicacy is revered all over the Far East. Today, we would dine like kings and I will exact my revenge.

Fun was had by all. The rice wine flowed and there was even Sake wine too. The guys had their brown tar Heroin, Pot and Coke too. Captain Davis was being his usual obnoxious self and now knowing his secret rendezvous, I ducked out of the festivities to set my trap.

In a monarchy, there will always be the loyal, as opposed to the ever friendly subordinate that lies in wait for your demise, when the opportunity arises. Those loyal are always few, while the character saboteurs are plenty. I discovered early on that anyone low enough to turn on anyone, even family, for a small reward would tell Mother Mary on Jesus for an even larger reward.

My promise of rank promotion opened many a man's mouth as to Kim Lings many lovers. I even found out she knew of my brief time with her mother. It would seem a negative word about me, would be the key that unlocked and parted her legs.

The Enemy Within

It would also seem she chose a field of death trees, because no one in their right mind would go in that area. There was no antidote for the trees deadly inhabitants; the dreaded 3 step Viper. I guess the thrill of death by snakes, mixed with me catching her in the act, was exciting to them. I made sure to do just that. Excite, then kill the both of them.

The plan was simple; spray the area trees; all but the one those lovers used, with Agent Orange. The harsh defoliant would kill trees, grass and any living thing in its wake. This done, I returned to the now drunken jungle boogie. The pretty girls danced, while everyone enjoyed the music and merriment. Soon we drifted off to our huts, when someone cries out

"Where is Kim Ling"?

"Yes, where is my wife", I ask "Find her and do it now". "This doesn't feel right".

Lynch and Davidson, along with me helped ourselves to another helping of the garlic spiced meat, until we heart the yell.

"They're here, they're here, Oh my God, come fast".

Finishing our food, served on giant plant leaves, we arrived to find Captain Davis naked and quite bloated with numerous snake bites and a horrified naked Kim Ling frozen in fear. The Vipers were all around her, waiting for her to move.

"Joe, I love you, I really do. He made me do this, I swear it Joe. I was in fear for my life, that's why we fucked".

"You fucked yourself, you filthy animal", I said as the others left in disgust. Then I felt the tap, tap, tap on my shoulder. It was Lynch again.

"Sir, time to move out. The men are with you".

"Merry Christmas Bitch"!

The Enemy Within

The morning following Captain Davis and Kim Ling's untimely deaths, was grim indeed. That is for the deceased. It would seem in everyone's state of drunken abandon, there was downright disgust for Kim Ling and her lover, Captain Davis, so their bodies were left in the field overnight. What the maggots didn't eat, the indigenous creatures of the night carted off. Quite possibly even for the nourishment of their young. The daytime feasting festivities that Christmas, so it seemed, continued into the night, by the nocturnal creatures. As I revel in this gruesome news, I ask

"Where is Lynch and Davidson"?

"Skirmish in the North, and they said they will return for you in a fortnight".

"A fortnight"? What am I, English all of a sudden"? Anyway, "Pip, pip ad tally ho" I say. "Tell me more about Kim Ling's horrible death and where is my wine and breakfast"? I have to feed this hangover.

Eating roast pork and fish, I marvel in the Eastern cuisine. As I look at all of the "once" overweight men, now trim and fit, I wonder why Americans in the West think that breakfast has to consist of eggs, bacon and potatoes, with toasted bread? A meal such as that is nothing short of poison. Poison it might be, but what I'd give for a greasy spoon restaurant's grease filled fries and side of bacon and sausage, eggs over easy and whole wheat toast, heavy on the butter. My thoughts on belly bombers and caloric suicide were interrupted by an endless procession of well-wishers. The men wished me well, even though most couldn't look me straight in the eyes. My God, I thought, how many men did that whore sleep with anyway? The women, along with endless dishes of food, said she wasn't worth it and they had a cousin, sister, and even a mother to take care of poor me. Yes, sympathy and bereavement were in abundance, as planned, but where was the loyalty, I so desperately wanted and above all demanded.

The time would come when the test of the devoted would raise its ugly head. I knew men, like sheep for the most part, like to be guided. Like the sheep, they look to their strong leaders to do just that.

The Enemy Within

Once again, my thoughts were interrupted by the sad tale of Kim Ling's missing body and only her arm was left. They gave me the gnawed off arm and I envisioned it making a useful cup holder and back scratcher! Captain Davis, it seemed, went to hell in shame. All of his body was missing, but his franks and beans. I don't know why the vermin of the night didn't eat his private parts. I guess even animals have standards?

Those few days were filled with memories and reflections of happier days with Kim Ling. Now the village insists I settle down and move on. Oh boy, bring on the babes!

The jungle yields enough nourishment to sustain most life forms. The indigenous made an art of straw, bamboo, and thatch huts, with little heat. This, however, with all that humidity and not to mention rainy seasons, that left most of us home bound. If I wanted to swim, I'd jump in a fuckin river. I hated that rain and this was also the breeding season for the obvious reasons.

So here I am, at home, along with my beautiful wife's hand. I amused myself with thoughts of using it as an implement of masturbatory pleasure. Yeah, what was left of Kim Ling was her monkey spanker. Oh Lord! I need a woman and I need one fast. VC jungle whores were off limits, unless you wanted a good dose of Viet Nam clap. This form of jungle VD would rot your dick from inside out.

With the return of summer and the supply chopper, my prospects looked good. Fresh canned goods and k-rations of spam were welcomed. The women and children loved the American chocolate. Generators, clothes and electronics and just about anything else we needed, the US Government sent. Everything that is, except an offer to return home. They wanted us to accept and stay in our new home. As we unloaded the big bird, Davidson said

The Enemy Within

"Sir, here she is".

"Who are you talking about"? I ask.

"Kelly Ling, Kim Ling's young sister. She came to wed you Sir".

"What the hell", I yell, "happy days".

As Kelly Ling stepped off the chopper, I could swear she was a clone of Kim Ling; that is, a younger one. Much thinner and short hair, I saw the Western influence. She was not VC and "Oh no", here goes that gut feeling again. Unlike her sister and mother, she spoke perfect English.

"Hello Joe, I've heard wonderful things about you and the camp".

"Did you happen to hear how we can get out of here in one piece"? I ask.

Davidson interrupts and says "Sir, meet Judy Taylor and Donna Smith, they were sent to give you a medical evaluation".

As Davidson delivered his introductions, I notice Kelly Ling intensely eyeballing me and the surrounding area. The new guest Doctors, Taylor and Smith, I knew straight away were CIA. Only what as their true mission? Kelly Ling however, as beautiful as she was, gave me the worst gut feeling. Another feeling I couldn't escape was the sexual butterflies I now felt, after a season without the touch of a woman. As I stared at her, I notice she had beautiful petite hands, like her sister. Caught in a stare down with Kelly Ling, the CIA scum doctors went on and on until Davidson speaks up and says

"Sir, blessed is the man that endures temptation".

This said, "Let's go to my place, I've prepared dinner" I say.

Walking to the hut, I quietly ask Davidson his knowledge of the obvious CIA operatives and the where-abouts of Lynch. Without looking at me, his only answer was to hand me yet another Bible and say

"Lynch will be here when we need him and pray, because the Devil has many faces".

The Enemy Within

As he spoke those words, my eyes met Kelly Lings and for a brief second, they seemed as black as coals. Noticing my uncomfortable gaze, she approaches and takes my hand and says

"Joe, I know what you just went through with Kim Ling and I am so sorry, but now I'm here and I want you to be open minded and hearted enough to give me a fair chance".

As her words warmed me over, her cold clammy hands brought my lonely sex starved senses back to reality. As I withdraw my hand, in this uncomfortable situation, I ask

"Kelly Ling, I was surprised because Kim Ling didn't mention family, only her mother".

"I was in America Joe, with my education. Now I've returned to do what I must for my country".

"Which country"? I ask.

"Which country are you currently helping Joe"? As she stares me directly in the eyes.

This educated, strong and unfortunately confronting woman was the opposite of her tight lipped sister.

"What country do I serve"? "The united republic of Joe, of course", I say as we reach my hut.

Davidson enters first with supplies and I notice the Pierre Cardin luggage the Doctors had. Thanks to the over-priced Pierre Cardin French name, but made in China crap they called fashionable, stuck out like sore thumbs. Davidson, I noticed saw them also and nodded in accord. As the women enter the hut, I eyeball them from head to toe. All were beautiful and I envisioned sex with each one. Kelly Ling sees my obvious lustful gaze and in a jealous tone says

"Take a picture it'll last longer".

This said, she steps in and looking at her also, I can't find a panty line and blurt out "Panties"?

Her reply was a smile and "sometimes".

The Enemy Within

I said to myself, I'd find out soon enough. Entering the hut, my guests were more than impressed with my jungle décor. The furniture resembled American Mid-West, only with a bamboo flavor. As everyone got settled, Kelly Ling cried out and everyone quickly entered the bedroom. Kelly Ling points to the severed arm that was holding a bottle of lotion. Looking at it and pointing

"What's that, its sacrilege"!

"No it's not, it's my monkey spanker"! I answer.

Pointing to a ring still left on one of the fingers, she says "And this"?

"Oh, just a ring", "Isn't that Jergens lotion something else"? "My monkey spanker is softer than a babies' bottom".

"That's sick", the doctors say leaving the room.

Kelly Ling only gives me a serious stare and also leaves.

Dinner was good, consisting of shrimp stew with orange flavored buffalo strips on a bed of lettuce. The wine was American whiskey, courtesy of my guests. Like most women, the doctors drank me under the table and kept up the pace. When the pot was brought out, Davidson politely excused himself and refusing to partake in any sinful activity. What was so sinful? I thought, as he left.

Doctors Taylor and Smith were pretty high and dancing in their under ware, while Kelly Ling only nursed her single drink. I didn't know or care what she or Davidson thought, I got three hot chicks and someone was getting lucky this night. Wishful thinking, as I was soon passed out and put to bed by Kelly Ling. Awakened by the touch of Kelly Ling a few hours later, I go into auto sex mode and try the old roll over.

"Not tonight Joe", she says and that's alright with me, because I was still so stoned in the morning, I'd only ask,

"Did we and did I enjoy it"?

The Enemy Within

Sunrise came with the familiar sensation of cold steel to my head. The doctors stood there with the gun and said

"Where is Lynch Joe"?

"Why"? I ask and what is the gun for"?

"Sorry" was all she said. Kelly Ling pumped across me to protect when "Click" nothing. "Click, click" the gun didn't fire, even though both women with two guns tried in vain to kill Kelly Ling and me!

"No, no Kelly ling screamed as she used her panty clad body to shield me.

I don't know why, but through all of this I looked up and spied the shotgun muzzle of Davidson's pointed at us.

"Always use a back-up and no Hun, I'm sorry, I said as I heard:

"The Lord giveth and the Lord taketh away". "Boom, boom".

Only for the first time Davidson didn't kill them, he blew their gun toting arms off. Now in the doorway, Davidson says as the armless women run out:

"Be gone, Satan and never cross this threshold again".

Kelly Ling says "Oh Joe, are you OK"?

Then and there, I knew what Davidson meant; the loyalty was at home, in the form of Kelly Ling. That is, for how long, I thought.

"Thank you, Kelly Ling. I'll never forget this".

Just then, Davidson with the two arms says

"Goodnight Sir, I'll get rid of this".

Laughing, I say, "Here, you can have this one too, handing him my monkey spanker. I won't need it any more. Enjoy yourself". Kelly Ling says.

"He better not"! "Tonight we will love and tomorrow we will talk".

The Enemy Within

FIRE FROM THE SKY

That night we did love and talk. Kelly Ling held nothing back and gave herself to me completely. She reminded me of her mother Kim Ling, even though I really didn't get to experience her true pleasures. I couldn't help but to think of all the other women in the eve of lustful relations with me and how the candle of time extinguished not only the love, but the very sight of them. Kelly Ling was too young to understand this psychosis and even though her culture dictated subservience, I knew her Western teachings could possibly change all that in an instant. For now, however, could a helpless romantic not fall for the woman that would give her life for me? That kind of devotion I knew only existed in India. When the husband was set adrift on his burning bed, his grieving wife would, in a state of hysteria, cast herself upon the burning embers to follow him to his hereafter. Wow, I heard of taking a bullet for someone, but that manner of devotion was, you might say, to die for.

I got to know Kelly Ling and saw a lot of similarities between us. Or was she doing what every woman on good behavior did to snag a man? That night saw first-hand the loyalty, I so desperately needed; the obsessive desperation that drove me to the murder of her cheating ass sister, Kim Ling. Paranoia mixed with my liquor and drugs didn't help my sense of longevity, but one thing I did know, God promises no one tomorrow, but today He gave me Kelly Ling. That was enough for me. Tomorrow I'd worry about the evil seed of fleeting love. God save this one, I prayed, as the time went on. She, for some reason, didn't want kids. Yet, even though we were wed immediately, this with Kelly Ling's air of mystic, kept me guessing.

Lynch told me to worry about the more important issues at hand. One being the systematic skirmishes inside the DMZ. The Cong were, as we knew, a constant threat, but as a result of our group of conscientious objectors, we were often attacked by not what I call "friendly fire". It was, as I saw it, pure unadulterated murder. I knew that when Lynch and Davidson went out on their skirmishes, it was nothing more than to stave off the enemy. Friendly or not. Both were deadly.

The Enemy Within

As this agony raised its ugly head over and over, again I found strength in Lynch and my trusty bottle of booze. Lynch's eyes, I could no longer look directly into and Davidson prayed for me with Bible verses and words of hope. Kelly Lings love protected me, but her eyes didn't lie. When I pressed her for the truth that I hid from myself, she told me to sober up and look inside for the truth that was covered by my lost dignity. The pressure of truth overbearing, it was time to sober up. Truth as in life has many faces, the pretty ones we love and like to be around. The ugly truth however, so many don't like to face. My way of avoiding confrontational anger was to immerse myself into an alcohol and drug state of oblivion. So now, with Kelly Ling's words, cutting my conscience and my own heart, stabbing at my very soul, the choice was obvious. Surrender to the everlasting sleep of suicide or sober up and rejoin the truth of the war of life.

I choose to fight, not only for myself, but for my peers. My A type personality wouldn't allow me to step down or check out, because power, like a sweet wine, intoxicates. All my life, in the business world, I relished the demise of my enemies. War and battle outcomes all rely on man's ability to out-maneuver his opponent through cunning strategy, and life mirrors this too. My weapons were my love and right hand men. Kelly Ling had combat experience and when I jokingly asked her

"What side she was on"?

She would always ask me what side I was on.

My new gift that Christmas was the new M-16 combat rifle. This new toy from Mattel toy weapons manufacturing didn't match up to the Russian AK-37, but it was more accurate. The ironic thing was every time I opened a new box of ammo, I expected to find a Barbie or Ken doll.

The Enemy Within

The time came for us to pack up for an early light departure. That night we talked of finding our way back to the US and some spoke of not returning at all. So with that element of death and fear in the air, I announced that any day is a good day to die, but tonight we will eat, love and drink to life. If God willing, tomorrow we will dine in hell! I ate well and loved Kelly Ling hard, to her promise she wouldn't let any harm come to me. Lynch and I laughed at the prospect of her protecting me, but little did I know? Pressure wasn't placed on anyone to join in the "fight or flight" as many called it. With my wife in agreement, we were going to make it back to New York.

Two years had passed since I was in a war zone, but came to the conclusion that either the Cong and or U.S. would kill us eventually. We would die fighting for freedom and kill for a flight to New York. So here we are, once again, not professionals, but a group of people in search of not the American way, but the way to America. We knew they wanted to firstly keep us here, and now with our desire to return home, they wanted us dead. Why? We would ask as we assembled our 20 or so men, women and one child; a six year old boy Kelly Ling cared for when his family was killed by the Cong for feeding Americans.

Little Ping Lou was used by his Viet Cong parents to deliver supplies to the hidden underground VC. This little bugger knew the jungle like his own back yard. Ping could spot hidden tunnels that Lynch would miss and could also use a firearm better than any soldier. He was very useful and his adopted mother, Kelli Ling, kept him at her side and showered him with love, like her own son.

Another addition to our group was brother Earl, from Jamaica. Brother Earl smoked pot like cigarettes, yet he was never stoned. A weapons specialist and just as good a scout as Lynch. He could spot an ambush or booby trap from 500 yards away.

The Enemy Within

That night, I slept early, knowing that the morning light would end my jungle vacation of sorts and return me to the reality of civilization. The morning lights never came due to the arrival of Lynch at my bedside. Tap, tap, tap on my arm brought me out of a sound sleep to the

"Sir, it's time to move out ASAP"!

Did Lynch just say ASAP? I asked, rubbing the sleep out of my eyes and covering Kelly Ling's panty clad body with the covers.

"Listen to the jungle Sir, just listen".

I did listen and heard silence. No monkey, no birds, and none of the other animal chatter I had grown accustomed to. Oh no, that gut feeling again. In an instant, Kelly Ling's eyes met with Pings and they jumped up in panic, dressing quickly. Turning to Lynch, I ask

"What the hell is going on"?

Little Ping yells "Fire from the sky, fire from the sky".

The sheer terror in Kelly Ling's eyes told me what her mouth couldn't.

Davidson, while quickly helping to collect our things, runs from the hut yelling

"The end is here, the end is here; flee all ye faithful, flee all ye who wish to survive".

All of this shit was too much for me and turning back to Lynch, he said

"Animals are the first to know when typhoons or hurricanes come. The animals take to the hills hours and sometimes days in advance".

Davidson cuts in and says "The Lord protects the innocent".

Kelly Ling runs from hut to hut yelling to

"Get out, get out, they're coming to kill us".

Running from the village, I ask Lynch

"How will they come"?

He replies, "Most likely by air, mortar shelling or Napalm".

The Enemy Within

Mortar shelling can ravage a village by blowing it to bits, but the fire from the sky was Napalm. This bomb was the simple, but effective invention from the DuPont Chemical Company. In layman's terms, the ingenious ingredients were gasoline and oil. When this fire gel gets on you, your first reaction would be to wipe or beat it off, but that would only spread the fire gel. Third degree burns or death were imminent. One bomb would ignite an entire block.

All I could think of was to protect my family and run as fast as possible. All didn't run or even leave for that matter, and then we heard the rumble of the approaching aircraft. We made it about a half a mile before the bombs started dropping the deadly Napalm. The few of us could only cower in the dirt, as we heard the screams and smelled the flesh of the burning dead. As the fireball approached us, I thought only water could save us. I was wrong, as once again, Kelly Ling threw herself across my body as she screams out

"Ping, Ping, where is my baby"?

As our deaths were moments away, I hold Kelly Ling to me and looking into each other's crying eyes say

"I love you and today is a good day to die".

With this said, Davidson says "Blessed are the followers of the Lord".

Into the base of a tree, little Ping was waiting with open arms for his mother. Davidson stayed outside, holding the trap door open as we piled in, just before the fire ball hit. We held each other tight, not knowing how many would survive. As the heat wave passed us, the earth's natural mud and soil protected us. It was Brother Earl that now told me

"That oil burns on water and going that route would have surely killed us".

"Ok, ok", I say, "Where's Davidson and Lynch"?

"They didn't enter Sir, someone held the trap door secure".

The Enemy Within

Kelly Ling and many others wept uncontrollably over the loss of Lynch, Davidson and their loved ones that were burned to death in the fireball. I was saddened too, but in my heart, I knew of two that God saved.

Exiting the secret tunnel that Ping had found to shelter us, we discovered the area littered with the charred remains of the people that chose not to leave on their own, but were forced to, once the fire drove them out. With nowhere to turn or hide, their only recourse was to surrender to death. And die they did, nothing was left. The Napalm laid waste to everything living. As usual, Lynch and Davidson were MIA, but during our talks, the days before, we knew our plans. The only problem was how do blacks, whites, and browns hide in a country that's yellow? Shit! This one was going to be hard.

Gathering ourselves, I said we had to push on, because we knew the cleanup forces were sure to come as soon as the area cooled off. Their objective was to seek and destroy with no prisoners. These orders to execute with extreme prejudice, were given only to a select breed of men. Women, children, and anything that moved, had to be killed. This, they did without giving it a second thought, unlike the new breed of soldiers that had to do drugs to do the same.

We were used to the horrors of war and this harsh jungle, so for us to get ourselves together pronto, was no problem. I was quick to learn that war, just like prison, was no place to mourn. In both cases, one had to be strong, in order to survive.

"Go, go, go", I yelled "head west".

The Enemy Within

Kelly Ling scooped up little Ping and all the supplies they could carry. All I could think of was weapons and ammo, because I knew the jungle would feed us plenty. The jungle was as quiet as a church, except for the sounds of branches, as we tore through the thick of it, as fast as we could. What a sight this was; men, women, and even a few children running, not like professional soldiers, but like the horrified people we were; more like lambs from the slaughter. I knew any run of the mill tracker could follow us blindfolded, but Lynch said to head west and I trusted him with my, or should I say, our lives. The jungle was empty, due to the air strike and that opportunity we would use over and over again. For days, we would use the massive complex network of tunnels, rivers and whatever means necessary to navigate west.

We didn't have a concrete plan of escape, but we knew that we somehow had information or something the government didn't want exposed in America; something important enough to silence us for good! This night, we would sleep in an abandoned ammo tunnel. The decision to rest was welcomed by all of us, due to the bloody sores and rashes, caused by the Agent Orange chemicals we had been exposed to, from head to toe.

Another advantage of tunnels and caves was the rodent abundance. To the West, this was gross, but to the East and hungry people in general, rats were quite the tasty morsel. Tonight, we ate rice and the other meat with cabbage. We were satisfied, but in pain. Our own urine was enough to stave off infections and with the absence of water, dirt baths would rid our bodies of small lice and larger leaches. Custom was to eat anything that moved, but even I drew the line when it came to the blood sticks. Those were the plentiful leaches and to snag a bird was like eating chicken.

Problems arose by going to the toilet in the bush, because our urine ammonia left signature traces. These odors were easily detected by the Americans using the Huey Choppers with sniffers.

The Enemy Within

Only two choppers were being used and we grew accustomed to the distinctive sounds of the engines. The Russians felt that bigger is better and when their CH-47 Chinooks came, you could hear them from miles away. They carried troops to boot. When we heard the American Bell manufactured Huey choppers, we had minutes to vacate because they were scouts for ordinance strikes. That's all it took for them to spot, then radio in, then get the hell out of there, because the bombs were on their way for the unlucky slobs that didn't leave. Tonight, the slow hum of choppers woke us and all we could do was to wait as they swept the area in their familiar pattern, looking for troops or the other enemy – us! Knowing that we hid and buried all of our waste in underground tunnels, we pushed on anyway.

Not far from the cave, came a loud crying sound of a baby. I had seen this trap a dozen times, but Kelly Ling felt different about the situation. Brother Earl knew the baby cried for food, but was rigged with a booby trap.

"Keep moving", I said without giving it much thought.

"Why, to kill another American"? He said

"Fuckin right! The very ones that are tracking or leading us".

This said, I yell "Kelly Ling, no", as she disarms the bomb.

"Joe, the child is innocent and doesn't deserve to die". She said, looking at Brother Earl.

I ask "Something in my gut tells me something else is wrong with the child".

Then out of nowhere Tap, tap, tap, on my shoulder; here is Lynch.

"Sir, we best be moving out, because the Cong expected to hear that bomb. Now a scout will return to investigate why it didn't go off".

I think to ask where he had been, when Davidson speaks from his treetop advantage.

 "Blessed are the children of the Lord. Here is the bomb they'll be listening for Sir". He tosses a mine into the distance to a loud explosion.

The Enemy Within

Lynch looks directly at me and says "Babies aren't good for anybody in the combat zone".

With Kelly Ling holding the child to her bosom and her M-16 rifle, she and the others move out with mean looks.

Brother Earl shakes his head as he falls in "This is bad shit man, Bad shit"!

And No, it was worse shit. That loud mouth baby didn't shut the hell up. Sugar, food, nothing could silence loud mouth. How we made it to the next tunnel, I don't know, but we did. Every man wanted to drop off the loud mouth, but we knew the VC would use him again as a booby trap. The poor kid was, for sure, a goner, but the women wouldn't see it. Now, here we were in a tunnel, underground, hiding with loud mouth, screaming his head off.

What could go wrong? Why, everything of course. Not to mention the passing VC patrol lookout Davidson said would be upon us in about 15 minutes. I turn to Kelly Ling and beg her to

"Get the child out of here, before he gets us all killed".

The other women felt as long as he was sleeping, no harm would come to anyone. Lynch turns to me and says

"Who's in charge, anyway"?

This bickering went on right until the first VC started to pass by us. Sitting there, my mind drifted to how ingenious the VC were at hiding their tunnels. They were next to impossible to spot or find. A broken tree branch, a dead animal, or even a series of stones gave locations to tunnels. An untrained eye wouldn't notice. As I sat thinking how smart we were at using the enemy's tactics. I was snapped out of my daydream by bigmouth's crying. Turning to my wife, Kelly Ling, all I could do was to stare at her and the baby. In desperation, she did all she could do, while crying.

The Enemy Within

Seconds felt like hours and now everyone looked to me for an answer. And with that, I looked to Lynch to solve the very problem that could get us all killed before we could even find out why, they wanted us dead. In a flash, I grabbed Kelly Ling and even faster Lynch took hold of the baby's neck and gave it a quick twist. There was a loud "pop", then silence. Baby big mouth would cry no more. With his neck broken, he would cry and suffer from whatever pain he was in, no more. As Kelly Ling held little Ping in her arms, they, along with many others cried in silence. Davidson took the lifeless baby in his arms and whispered,

"The Lord giveth and the Lord taketh away".

Handing the baby to Kelly Ling, I say

"You know the needs of many outweigh the needs of a few.

"Kelly Ling, Lynch had no choice."

Still crying and now clear of troops, above, she says

"I know Joe, just promise me no harm will come to little Ping".

Looking at Lynch, my thoughts raced. Yes, little Ping could find a tunnel faster than any of us, including Lynch, and Kelly Ling loved him as her own. Would I let him or anyone else compromise our safety? Would I lie to a woman and tell her what she wanted to hear? Looking to Lynch for a lie or even a way out, he only lowers his head. Looking at Davidson, he predictably says

"Put it in the Lord's hands".

Looking back to Kelly Ling, I lie, "No harm will come to little Ping, as long as I live, I promise".

With the deception behind me, I find my mind racing again, back to happier times with Kelly Ling at the camp. I asked her many times why she didn't want to conceive and she could only say

"Not in war". With the orange sickness and flu, we all suffered, a baby would be too taxing on her, I guessed.

The Enemy Within

Then back to reality, Tap, tap, tap on my shoulder was Lynch.

"Sir, time to move out. If we hump it all night, we can make camp at daylight by Gator Lake".

"Why Gator Lake"? I ask.

Lynch smiles through his slits for eyes. "Because it's too dangerous to enter; that's where we can wash and camp".

I figure who can argue with logic and by now, our sores were on fire with the Orange. Dirt could only help so much and the constant urine wipes made all of us smell like street bums. Gators or not, we needed water. What we couldn't get from the morning dew, we got naturally from ourselves. We drank our own urine in order to survive. Imagine, as hungry as we were, was a fuckin Gator was going to eat us? Hell no, we were excited like going out to dine.

"Just like home", I said to Kelly Ling,

"First, we wash, then we eat a feast; Gator – yum, yum".

Trek, we did, all night long with the thoughts of a rewarding sparkling wash and drink of river water. Oh God, I thought, what have we become?

Arriving out of the thick at first light, we marveled at the beauty of the water and the waterfall.

"How can this beautiful place be so dangerous", I asked Lynch.

"Look" was all he said as he tossed a live rat in the water. In a second the serene waters turned into a violent state of a feeding frenzy. It seemed a million Gators were trying to eat one little rat.

"How will we do this", I asked.

"Just like down home Alabama. They eat their own as fast as they'll eat us".

"Watch and whatever you do, no gun fire to give away our position".

The Enemy Within

Going into his pocket, he pulls out a silencer and puts it on his colt 45. Putting another rat on a string, he throws it into the shallows and when they come after it, he pulls it in and pop, pop, two gators were shot in the head. The others scattered when their buddies were killed.

"Pretty smart critters". I said.

The women went to work on the animals, saving the hide for water containers and the meat for the long awaited feast. The men fashioned together 3 rafts using trees and bamboo for rope. The hide water bags were used to wash us and most looked like lepers by now. Plant sap was applied to our sores and we went on with it. A few fish were even caught using gator meat bait, by my southern woodsmen friends Davidson and Lynch. Some of our local guest VC laughed at Lynch's fishing, because they said it was a waste of precious meat. The VC would use children to snatch the fish out of the water with scoop bamboo sticks. When I asked

"What about the kids", they would say "we're not stupid, we use only the girls; no loss".

Eastern traditions aside, we ate better than we did in months. While doing so, I whispered to Lynch.

"How long were you going to wait to tell me someone is giving away our position, over and over again"?

"When I knew for sure". Was his only answer.

"You always know for sure Lynch. What are they doing to us man"?

"They're picking us off, slowly, but surely!

"Hey man, I know you're here to protect us, but I need to know will my wife and I live through this". For the first time, Lynch's eyes filled with tears. Getting up and walking away, he says,

"Sir, we all died long ago, and your traitors will reveal themselves soon enough".

"Lynch, Lynch, damn it man, tell me more. Don't leave me hanging like this". "Who's dead? What dead? What the fuck"? "I noticed you didn't use gender in your suspects".

The Enemy Within

Davidson steps in and says

"Trust in the Lord, Sir, our Judas will reveal himself at daybreak".

Looking to Kelly Ling for answers, she looked up from her task of grilling the gator meat and said

"Joe, you, along with all of us trust Lynch. Trust him now, we stand behind you and I know you stand behind him. Come and eat".

Finding a secluded spot to enjoy my family and food of roasted gator tail; garlic rat tips; smoked fish with swamp salad. Lynch said in the South, the wild grass or swamp salad was called swamp cabbage. This cabbage was very good and we even had a dessert of sugar cane pulp. The meal was very good and for the first time in months we didn't eat to kill the pain of hunger, we ate to content.

The children were cautioned to stay away from the water's edge and the adults caught up on their rest. Kelly Ling slept in my arms, as I could only drift off to better times. I remembered my holiday pick nicks in New York City. Even though concrete city offered little to no grass, my friends and I would go down to the East River Drive and roast a pig Spanish style, while our girl friends would prepare rice and beans. We drank more Budweiser beer than we drank water, and true to Puerto Rican custom, a lot of cocaine and even more heroin was consumed all day long, among the men. Then we would pair off and make love to our girlfriend's and wives. We would use the excuse of beer runs to cop more drugs, because our girls said we did too much.

Looking around now, I thought how my current company's drug use was to kill the pain of death and numb the pain of the Agent Orange sickness. Heroin, pot or whatever pain killer we were on, one pain couldn't be killed: Blue balls!

The Enemy Within

Between the Cong, Americans and every venomous snake in the jungle, trying to kill us, making love to Kelly Ling didn't cross my mind too much. Our sores left our outer appearance leper like and tender was the painful touch. Gentle we were in the seclusion of the bush. The jungle hid us well and I tried to hide as much of myself inside Kelly Ling's silky bush. The rapture I felt couldn't compare to my love for her. Nothing else in the world East or West mattered at this moment. In the bliss of love, I thought, what could be better than a full stomach and empty balls? Money perhaps? Quite possibly, but for now, nothing but my Kelly Ling. We made up for lost sleep, talk, loving and I simply reveled in just the touch of a woman's flesh.

Kelly Ling admitted to me that the Americans constant medical contact with us was unusual and she was sure that Lynch and Davidson knew more than they let on. We both agreed that it was a "big business war" and somehow big business had a lot to do with our predicament.

That night, we cornered Lynch with the questions we so desperately needed answers to. Lynch said "it was a business war", but it was our business to get out ASAP and the morning light would bring us the answers and escape, we all so desperately longed and died for.

The 0400 alarm that awoke me this morning, wasn't that of an alarm clock or even a jungle rooster. This morning brought in the alarming shouts of a furious Jamaican. With no clocks to silence, in a sleep drunken panic, I dressed in seconds and armed myself even quicker. Looking around, Kelly Ling was gone, so I could only follow everyone else that followed Brother Earl's screams of panic. With not enough time to fully come to our senses, we ran as we dressed like drunks.

The Enemy Within

In no time, we reached the river's edge to find Brother Earl's state of alarm. In the three rafts, were little Ping and most of our Company. Frozen in fear, shock and bewilderment, I couldn't believe my sleep drunk eyes. With Little Ping in the lead, they were paddling as fast as they could to get away, not from the VC, or the Americans, but us! Filled now with rage, I raised my M-16 and took aim, only to feel the tap, tap, tap on my shoulder from none other than Lynch,

"Don't shoot Sir," he said.

Davidson spoke up and said "The devil is a liar and the truth will prevail".

Kelly Ling held out her hand that was full of American dollar bills.

"I found this last night, as I packed little Ping's things and Lynch told me to wait. Joe, we waited and watched all night to see just who was working with the Americans. Now we know".

Brother Earl raised his weapon and said, "I'll kill 'em all".

When Davidson and Kelly Ling said "just wait" With that said, little Ping opened his back pack and took out handfuls of dollars and chocolate bars.

Kelly Ling said "Why Ping, why?"

Laughing, Ping only says "You Americans came and destroyed our country, and our homes and families. Now I will destroy you".

Kelli Ling sternly says "Ping, you must return now and we will put all this behind us; please baby".

Her cries were answered by gun fire from the rafts. We dived for cover when Davidson spoke up and said

"The devil will soon claim his own".

Turning to Lynch, I ask him "What'll we do now and why are you smiling"?

Kelly Ling answers "Look Joe".

The Enemy Within

As little Ping continued his patriotic rant, he scoffed at us, and the hungry gators that followed closely behind. That is until they noticed the frayed bamboo bindings that were cut the night before, start to come apart. The gators also noticed and circled the rafts like Custer at the Alamo. Arrows and Tomahawks however, pale in comparison to death by hungry gators.

Now, panic stricken, Ping and his once defiant band of deserters tried in vain to hold the rafts together. As one man held the bamboo, a gator snapped his hand off! The blood that squirted all over the place made the gators even more aggressive. A gator with a very large head rammed into the last raft and the crash totally ripped the craft apart. Everyone fell into the water, but very few got wet. All that was heard was the awful sound of crunching bones.

The second raft wasn't as lucky. A quick death wasn't in store for them. As the people held on for dear life, a gator bit into a loose bamboo rope and towed the raft into the shallows where hundreds of baby gators waited to be fed. With a very loud bellowing sound, a large female seemed to tell the others to back off. And they did. As they left, she returned to the young gators. With one powerful blow from her 10 foot tail, the raft was in splinters and the people were in the now blood filled waters of hungry baby gators, getting their fill of people food. Seeing this, little Ping had a change of heart and as the gators moved in, he yells

"Mommy, mommy, help me please, help me, they made me leave you. I love you Mommy".

Kelly Ling couldn't watch and coldly turned to me and said

"We better be going now, because I know he told of our position".

Just then, shots rang out. The raft people chose a bullet to the brain, before being devoured by gators. Six out of seven people shot themselves right before the gators ate them. Little Ping was last to go. He gave us the finger and jumped in and swam towards the shore. He got close, but got no cigar. Two gators grabbed him and went into a death roll. This tore him in two! Two more gators grabbed him again and again, until that little tunnel rat bastard was no more.

The Enemy Within

I held Kelly Ling and even though she didn't watch, she saw it in my eyes, as I did.

"Are you going to be OK"? I asked.

"Yes Joe, but now we must ready ourselves for the chopper to take us home".

"What the hell are you talking about", I asked. Tap, tap, tap, was Lynch on my shoulder again. Senator Nixon is flying in to pick us up for debriefing, before our trip home Sir".

"And the gator river", I asked.

"It was the only way to let the enemy show himself even though there were more of them than we thought". I don't know about choppers". I said, "They have a habit of crashing."

We figured this "Lynch said as a rifle butt struck my head, knocking me out cold.

The Enemy Within

HOSPITAL OF DEATH

In my unconscious state, my mind drifted in and out of reality. This was nothing new to me, because ever since the exposure to the Orange jungle sickness, our nights and in severe cases, days were akin to bad LSD trips. Another means of sickness was the new armor piercing shell. The spent shells were very high in toxic radiation. Both gave the same results. Skin lesions, headaches, and the worst case being birth defects. We called the dreams, radioactive dreams. It was a dream and a terrible state of semi-conscious brain pain. Nothing was real, truths were lies, and reality was an elusive wind that could never be caught. Sleep, sleep, sleep was the only escape. Even as painful as it was. It's called sleep, but I can't say for sure, if any rest was accomplished in it. I could hear every sound, every word and I could awaken at will, only I didn't want to.

Escapism was the only true freedom in our world and mine was falling apart. Blood meant death, Orange meant a slow sickness and my dreams were black and grey. What did it mean? I thought as I listened for clues; the clues never came, but consciousness did with a cold splash of water. Running down my face, I found it also the cleanest I've had after in months in the bush.

Kelly Ling: "Joe, are you awake"? Are you OK? Wake up, wake up.

Looking around, I saw we were in a mash tent. The medical camp was packed full of mostly amputee soldiers that were unlucky enough to survive a bomb or mine blast. The new growing group was our tents of Orange jungle sickness.

Joe: "From what I've been hearing, I guess I'm going to make it. Baby, are you alright"?

Kelly Ling: "Yes Joe, Senator Nixon has us sign all the necessary forms and we'll be in Washington in a few weeks.

Joe: "Washington weeks? I just can't make it back to New York, can I?

The Enemy Within

Kelly Ling: "The only place capable of treating us is Walter Reed Hospital in Washington. Our new home is there too; we have to go to survive Joe. Please don't you leave me now."

Joe: "And my men"? Kelly Ling: "Sleep Joe, go to sleep".

I did sleep, and found that in a hospital setting, the abundance wasn't in pleasure and fun, but in agony and death. My men, the few that were left, were also sick. Our infections masked the real sickness. We did find that the ones that didn't use urine on themselves did smell better, but lost limbs, due to infection. Lynch and Davidson still came and went, but always came in for blood transfusions and some type of experimental treatment. It would seem we were all getting one form of treatment or another, but no one talked about it.

One night, I asked Brother Earl if he was going to return to Jamaica. He said the spirits told him he wouldn't make it back home and would I promise to send his ashes home? I promised that I would, then jokingly asked if the spirits said I'd make it. Seriously said that yes, I'd make it home to die. I didn't care, I only wanted to die on American soil, without people trying to kill me. I also wanted the truth behind this awful war and its post battle casualties that were dying all around me. Not from wounds, from time. I grew more and more impatient because time is this jungle wasn't a luxury we could afford. Now we knew that time was the enemy.

There were many enemies in my life and all wanted to take life. Another jungle sickness was the black plague. This death came from dirty, infected whores that deliberately gave the disease to soldiers. The telltale signs were skin lesions that began on the stomach and back, then crept up the back to the arms and neck. In the advanced cases, the face would be covered with the pot marks. The mash camp had a lot of orange and black sickness. The treatment for the Black Death was a plane ride, one way that is, to an island in the South Pacific. Like a medieval Leprosy colony, all that entered were rumored not to leave. It was also said that they had to be quarantined due to the contagious rate of growth.

The Enemy Within

Plague Island was the United States only means of recourse to keep the plague out. After risking life and a lot of limbs, a final blood test determined if you went home or stayed hidden away. There are many ways to die and I've survived ten years in a maximum prison, but this new immune system disease, could kill you from just a common cold, a cut, or anything else that could escalate into death.

One night, while showering, I noticed Brother Earl's back was covered with lesions.

Joe: "Brother Earl, what's up with your back man"? That shit looks serious.

Brother Earl: "I don't know man. This could stop me from going back home. Man, I don't want to die on Plague Island."

Joe: "If you go there, you know that none of your body parts can leave there".

Brother Earl: "Do you think we could make another escape"?

Joe: "Like here? Man we're not even out yet; notice that? We didn't escape shit yet"!

Brother Earl: "How does this shit spread"?

Joe: "They say from sex and cuts, sores, needles too. It's a virus".

Brother Earl: "What about kissing and mosquitos"?

Joe: "Kissing and mosquitos"?

Brother Earl: "Mosquitos are flying needles, and aren't viruses in saliva? That's how we spread colds right?"

Joe: "I don't know, Brother Earl. If they knew I don't think they'd tell us anyway".

Brother Earl: "You know we both have jungle rot on our bodies"?

Joe: "Yeah, so"?

Brother Earl: "So look at the blood we're standing in".

Looking at the shower floor, our rotted feet were in pools of blood from our bodies.

Joe: "Oh shit"!

The Enemy Within

The American mash doctors weren't completely heartless when it came to the wounded enemy. The camp was in a valley surrounded by hills. The enemy VC would fire grenades into the camp, risk their lives with bombs and snipers would target anyone they thought were brass. The VC women would also cook and clean for the compound and whoever had money. One quiet Sunday morning, while Kelly Ling and I were eating breakfast, off in the distance, we heard a baby crying.   Curious, we came to the front gate to find Brother Earl with gun drawn on the baby.

Brother Earl: "Stay away man, it's another bomb".

Kelly Ling comes with a doctor and gives Brother Earl that look again.

Brother Earl: "Kelly Ling, stay out of it. Joe, control your wife before she gets us killed".

Doctor: "Well, can anybody disarm it".

Brother Earl: Eyes were tear-filled when he spoke. "Sarg, Brother Joe, the spirits told me that today, I would join them; please, not like this".

Joe: "Please, no more mumbo-jumbo, hu-du, voo-doo stuff".

Doctor: "Well, if you idiot are not going to do anything, I'll just…

Everyone yell's at the Doctor "NO"! But he yanks the baby up to the horrific two second click of the timer.

Brother Earl: "All praise to Jah Rastafari".

Kelly Ling is pushed aside as Brother Earl throws himself into the path of the bomb blast. The bomb wasn't a large one, but it was a shaped charge, designed to go in one direction and Brother Earl took most of it, which just about tore him in two. The white coat caught a leg wound, began to cry like a woman, then started to run away, just like the fool he was.

Joe: "Brother Earl, why man, why"?

Brother Earl: "Jah Lord wanted me today, not you"

Joe: "Brother Earl, my beautiful war machine; who will protect us now"? My tears flowed like the jungle water falls.

The Enemy Within

Brother Earl: "I'm not broken down man, just out of gas". Holding my hand, he looks me in the eyes. Then, with his last breath.

Brother Earl: "We're all dead. You look after Lynch, Davidson and Kelly Ling. How about my ashes now?

Joe: "Brother Earl, I swear it will be done. We'll see you soon."

Brother Earl left me that day. As he died in my arms, my sadness turned to rage. I followed the doctor's trail of blood to an operating tent and as the shrapnel was removed from his leg, I emptied my 45 side arm into his gutless spine, by way of his stomach.

Joe: "Go to hell, you son of a bitch".

There was a court marshal and review boards, but how can you punish a dead man in a state of hysteria. I just didn't care. I did keep my promise to Brother Earl. We burned his body with diesel gasoline, because it burns longer and hotter. His ashes were shipped to Jamaica and he was awarded the Congressional Medal of Honor. We had a special service for him with Davidson, delivering a heartfelt sermon.

Something was wrong with Kelly Ling, since the death of Brother Earl. She didn't have much to say for days and I knew it had something to do with the baby that was saved from the VC mine. Determined to end her sadness, I found the baby and brought it home to our tent. At the sight of it, she broke down and cried uncontrollably.

Joe: "Kelly Ling, Kelly Ling, what's wrong"?

Kelly Ling: "I can't have children and these bitches are throwing them away".

Kelly Ling was mad and hurt that she couldn't have children of her own, due to her medical orange condition. Her eyes stopped crying and turned as I've seen on other occasions, black. Picking up her side arm in a trance-like mode she says "I'll kill that bitch".

Joe: "Kelly Ling, no, don't do it, please don't. Her answer didn't come in words, but a pistol to my head.

The Enemy Within

Once, I came to, I was seeing the usual stars, but the irony of it was, I was getting used to the head trauma. One thing I wasn't getting used to was Kelly Ling's big mouth and waning subservience. Lynch entered and said I should come immediately because Kelly Ling and a VC mama son were having a cat fight. Arriving in minutes, we see the women had an audience of cheering men. Reason was, as with any cat fight, they were already down to panties and bras. Kelly Ling's eyes were as black as coals, as she trashed about the room punching and screaming. Trying to yell for them to stop, I knew nothing short of a bucket of water could stop the wild women. This I'll never do that again, because now it felt like twenty sharp knife-like finger nails were tearing at me. I couldn't believe my eyes and tearing flesh. The wild cats were now turned on me!

The war brings so much frustration and pent up anxieties, and no one can cope in the same way. I told the boys and by now, a few female nurses, to back off and let the now bra less women vent their pain and hurt. Suddenly, a nurse turns to a guy and tears at him saying he was a creep and she hated him. A soldier sucker punches a sergeant in his mouth, shouting accusations of cruelty and war crimes. This hysteria and passions and anguish spread faster than the diseases the camp was treating. The doctors got it the worst, with the amputees beating everyone in sight with their artificial limbs, canes and crutches. The white coats were now red. I guess the men without anyone to bash had stepped outside. The carnage carried on inside.

Joe: "Hey Lynch, why didn't you pull those wild cats off of me"? Look at me, they tore me up!

Davidson: "Sometimes, words can't say how we feel".

Lynch: "Did you ever want to punch out your boss or a prison guard, but couldn't.

Joe: "Yeah, you're right. Think they are naked by now? Ha, ha, ha".

The Enemy Within

By morning light, the dust had settled and a peaceful calm was upon the camp. In the prior months, the tension was so thick, you could cut it with a knife. The rumors and pending diagnosis had everyone up tight. Pending slow death, or loss of limbs were the norm, but this day the sound of the birds and jungle was once again beautiful.

Even more beautiful was my wife, adorned in a flow and leaf halo and panties. Her floral head band and body resembled a Venetian Goddess. Passion abounds and once again I was reminded of my devotion for Kelly Ling and hers for me. That morning, we lay in loves bliss, talked about the future and reminisced in the past, that is, until her mother, Kim Ling was brought up. She told me I didn't help to save her life and I countered with "She was part of the VC and knew of the ambush to kill us. So yes, she was wounded in the skirmish". I didn't mention our ten second hokey pokey, leading to nowhere. Kelly Ling was OK with my explanation and we moved on. That subject was never brought up again.

Later that day, orders came for the camp to relocate, due to increased skirmishes and bombings. We were starting to become easier targets. Due to security issues, we were given last minute orders with only a day to break camp before the air strikes vaporized the area. Spirits were high and we were used to moving about the jungle.

Lynch: "Sir, I have some guys that want to meet you. Bobby-V, Tony-G and another Jackson.

Joe: "Another Jackson? You don't mean the Florida family of assholes".

Lynch: "I am afraid so, Sir".

Joe: "So guys, where do you hail from"?

Bobby-V: "We're from Philly Sir and we've heard a lot of good things you've done here and that's righteous".

Tony-G: "Yeah definitely".

Bobby-V: "Sir, if you don't mind we would like to tag along for the trip to the next camp".

Tony-G: "Yeah, definitely".

The Enemy Within

Joe looks at Lynch and he nods. "He say anything else"?

Tony-G "Sometime definitely".

Joe: "So Jackson, I had the misfortune of running into your family scum".

Jackson: "No Sir".

Joe: "Are you a sniveling coward"?

Jackson: "No Sir".

Joe: "Are you a turncoat mother fucker? I bet you are".

Jackson: "Sir, yes Sir".

Joe: "I almost forgot, idiots too".

Jackson: "Sir, my Momma, Daddy and all my aunties are proud of me".

Joe: (looking at Lynch) "Oh, no".

Jackson: "Sir, my Grandma said with my head, I'd be a Sergeant in no time".

Joe: "With your head you'd make a fuckin hat rack, you idiot".

Jackson: "Sir, yes, Sir".

Everyone stood and laughed at Jackson. I don't know if it was the drugs the white suits were pumping into me, but I saw something good in the kid and took a liking to him. Besides, he was strong as an Ox and the Orange had my bones, muscles, and joints hurting me like crazy. Jackson had the Orange sickness, like most of us, but at twenty and looking at a Florida ridiculous sixty year bid in prison, this jungle hell was not only better than prison, but also freedom. What he couldn't know then was, his freedom wouldn't last long.

The Enemy Within

The hardest part of moving a medical camp isn't the beds, the equipment, or even the supplies, it's the sick. The post medical care from the white suits was, as we didn't realize at the time, a prerequisite for V.A. care. That is, a very mechanical way of making you a number. Heading to higher ground, the roads, when we had the luxury of riding them, were bumpy and booby trap laden. The bush was worse with just about everything trying to kill you. The Orange had our bones and flesh on fire and not to mention the painful bumps that sometimes made just walking next to impossible.

Our trip was to take three days and nights. At the end of the first day, we could push on no further. Dash safety, dash orders and to hell with common sense, we were bunking down. The women prepared camp; K rations, as not to draw attention to our position. We did know that we were in their back yard and they knew every move we made. The question was, did they need non-combatants that were very sick. We made camp and ate the canned beef, block cheese and crackers.

Jackson: "I wish my Mama was here".

Lynch: "What the hell for".

Jackson: "to cook for me".

Bobby-V: "Hey Tony, do you remember Tammy from Hoboken? Man, she could cook some baked clams".

Tony-G: "No, that was Suzie the slut from Jersey City".

Bobby-V: "You mean Joe potato salads sister"?

Tony-G: "No, that was Tommy the Axe's cousin".

Joe: "What the hell are you guys talking about"?

Bobby-V: "Wait a minute, Stevie the blade's sister, back in Trenton"?

Tony-G: "Oh, I heard about that, didn't she cut her head off"?

Bobbie-V: "No, that was Louie the butcher, he used her head for his hog head cheese".

The Enemy Within

Joe: "Hog head cheese? What the fuck! What the hell are you guys on"?

Jackson: "If my Mama was here, she could make us some big boy dinners".

Joe: "Big boy dinners"? You fuckin idiot. How old are you"?

Jackson: "Sir, twenty five, yes Sir. My Aunties and Daddy say I'm too old for my age".

Joe: "Trust me Einstein, they were wrong."

This banter went on into the wee hours of the morning. Everyone eventually went to sleep with Kelly Ling and me slipping away for some alone time. In a secluded place, Kelly Ling and I elevated our passions to new heights. As I chased the elusive butterfly of love through Poppy fields, the planets were in perfect alignment. What we didn't realize, that Timothy Leary, LSD and Carl Saigon's planets couldn't prepare us for another one of the jungles hidden surprises. The camp was surrounded and the gunfire brought us tumbling back to earth.

Running back to the camp, we prayed to find survivors. I was mad as hell that the Viet Cong could stoop so low, as to attack a medical camp. Kelly Ling reminded me of the Viet Nam hospitals, schools, and other innocents that were killed daily. War crimes aside, we both agreed that in war, it's not who's right, but who's left.

There goes that gut feeling again. Arriving as fast as our sore feet could deliver us, the carnage that greeted us made Custer's last stand look like a formal dinner party. The regiment of men and core engineers thought, as we did, that medical camps as per the Geneva Convention, were off limits. This wasn't the case however. The ensuing blood bath left very few survivors. The means of attack always dictates the enemy's motives, and there aren't any good motives. These kind of attacks are made out of either revenge or needs, such as for food, or just an order from the top brass for whatever strategic reason they may have.   We didn't rape any village teen or raid a village innocents. They however, it would seem, needed medicine and provisions. They took everything and killed all that got in their way to do so.

The Enemy Within

Lynch and Davidson were helping the wounded and Davidson was sending off the dead.

Joe: "Lynch, where is Jackson"?

Lynch: "They got him Sir".

Joe: "What do you mean, got him? Is he a prisoner and why"?

Lynch: They do so to keep us away. Normally they take brass".

Joe: "Pack it up, we're out of here."

Bobby-V: "Sir, we can't leave the kid".

I looked around and their looks told me that that idiot Jackson also made an impression on them too. Turning to Lynch, I asked if he had a plan and he looked at the Philly boys and smiled through those slit eyes. We knew the Cong were also suffering from the Orange and Black plague and the Americans for some strange reason, though a new disease, were years into research and years ahead into treatments. Asking Lynch to reconsider, I was told that they would do the same for me. I replied that the kid was shit and I perhaps was selfish, but not shit.

Kelly Ling: "Joe, what's happened to you"?

Davidson: "Dignity lost can never be found".

Joe: "When do we go on"?

Tony-G: "You don't, me and Bobby will handle this".

Joe: "Alone"?

Bobby V: "Don't worry, we'll make 'em an offer they can't refuse".

Tony-G: "and we'll get back our medicine too".

When Lynch only smiled, somehow I knew all would be OK.

The Enemy Within

Compliance and a woman's love made me weak and deep inside I knew I had to regain my company's respect. Where does one find his lost dignity? I wondered. A dead martyr perhaps. I waited till everyone was asleep, that was after the sad farewells to follow the two Philly boys into the thick of it. After a few hours of walking and crawling through vegetation that cuts like a knife, was not new to us, so, by now I was a pro at it. I don't know about the jungles of the world, but the two Philly boys were straight out of a James Cagney movie, because their style was really gangster.

As the sentry walked his patrol route back and forth, Bobby-V out of nowhere pops up and asks for a light. The shocked soldier didn't have time to respond because Tony-G was behind him, pushing a bam-boo ice pick into the base of his head. Silently and swiftly, they made their way to the inner circle of the camp. Two soldiers sat outside a tent drinking rice wine, they were oblivious to the torture going on inside. Moving in closer to listen, I noticed the Philly boys were also listening to Jackson being shocked with a truck battery. This was typical and it sure beat the bam boo shards inserted into the fingernails. As bad as the scene went, all Jackson would yell was

"Fuck you and my Daddy is a gangster and would kill all of you gooks".

In the blink of an eye, Bobby-V was slowly pushing the bamboo pick into one's head, while Tony-G had fashioned a wire between two bamboo shoots to form a garrote. This poor gook slob was choked to a silent death. Then they did something that proved, once again, this place was full of America's worst. The boys screwed on silencers that they could have used all the time. They obviously liked killing people. When this was over, I made a mental note to find out what the hell these cold blooded murderers were locked up for in the first place? The candle light cast three shadows on the tent. The outside moonlight cast two, one shadow raised the gun to the shadow with the battery and silently blew his head all over the other shadow. One second later, reeling from the blood bath, the second shadow blows his eyeball out of its socket. The third shadow runs out of the tent and is greeted with a knife through the neck up to his brain. Now, no longer a shadow, the man drops to his knees and gags. Jackson exits the tent and kicks the end of the knife, driving it to the hilt into the enemy brain. I found it amazing that not a sound erupted from the killings going on before my eyes. These guys were good, but were they going to massacre the entire camp? Then, I feel the familiar tap, tap, tap, on my shoulder.

The Enemy Within

Lynch: "Sir, we should be moving out. The place will be crawling with VC soon.

Just then the Philly boys and Jackson showed up and asked me if I like the show. I said it was their

Sick pleasure, not a show!

Jackson: "There's only a few left. Why don't we finish them off"?

Joe: "I thought you were a thief, now you have a taste for blood"?

Jackson: "Sir, the tortured me, look at the burns on my body"!

Joe: "So you should kill all of them"? I'll tell you what, you're a thief, so I want you to steal all of our medicine and equipment back without a peep out of you and if you hurt a hair on anyone, well, let's just say you won't face the morning light. OK, you fuckin idiot"?

Jackson was more than happy to oblige, trip after trip to the bush he brought everything that wasn't nailed down. The few soldiers that were left never woke up and when they did, I don't know what they would eat, because we had everything.

Trekking back to our camp, I asked Jackson what was stuffed into his shirt and pockets. "Money, for my suffering Sir". Was all he said and I said, "Yep, you are a thief". Knowing a new platoon with a "kill all" mission would arrive in the morning, we packed to pull out.

Kelly Ling: "Joe, a chopper is going to lift us out".

Joe: "No way, don't trust em"

Tap, tap, tap! "Time to move out" Bang went the gun butt to my head again!

The Enemy Within

EPILOGUE

Slipping in and out of consciousness, I couldn't distinguish between reality and bad dreams. In some dreams, Kelly Ling was at my side holding my hand that was attached to an intravenous-filled arm, telling me she loves me and not to worry. Then to sleep. This said, a person in white clothes, like a doctor would come and operate on me, while I was awake. During these episodes, I had no conception of time and in my brief moments of clarity, nothing made sense to me.

Finally, one day, the warm sensation of sunlight on my face brought me to my conscious senses. As the fog slowly lifted from me, I knew just from the smell, I was in hospital. Kelly Ling held my hands as I said nothing, but tried desperately to mentally piece the past together. I remembered the chopper ride and even Senator Nixon promising to help us, as long as we signed the orders of confidentiality. I struggled to remember what was so secret, but couldn't. What I also couldn't do, because of the tubes was talking, pissing and everything else. I could however, moan and grunt. Any idiot would know I wanted answers. Kelly Ling spoke up, with those men in white suits next to her.

"Joe, you're very sick. We all are and the VA is going to take care of us. Soon you can come home to our new home".

What illness, I thought and what new home? Where was this home and where the hell was I anyway? All I could do was wait and listen. I did learn through my semi-sleep stages that I suffered from Agent Orange born cancers. Out of 21 various cancers it caused, I had 7. The doctors replaced the main arteries in my arms, legs and in my neck. The pain was unbearable and my days and nights were spent grunting for my morphine shots.

The Enemy Within

I was no stranger to opiates and my New York drug past left me with a very high tolerance to the opium I now needed. I heard the white suits say ten times the morphine, just to ease the pain. The only fun was the sponge baths by the large-breasted women in white. I found it very hard calling those doctors and nurses, due to their lack of professionalism and manners that paralleled an illiterate prison guard. Bedside manners, along with basic human rights didn't occur to these primates. One day, as the white suits spoke to each other, as if I wasn't even there, I heard that most of my "tubes" were to come out. Good, I thought, because now I could curse these mother fuckers out proper! Kelly Ling in all her wisdom, had other plans.

One of the first stage tubes to be removed was the catheter for my Johnson. It was painful as hell, but one pain was like any other, when that's all you know. As it was being removed, I saw the twinkle in Kelly Ling's eye and when she winked, I knew what was on her mind. Each day, she would come late and draw my bed curtain for privacy. With gentle hand manipulation, she masterfully gauged my pain and pleasure. Soon enough, once again things seems to be getting better, except that is for the constant itch on my leg that wouldn't go away. With months gone by and me not being able to talk, my grunts directed Kelly Ling to my legs to scratch. She did so and always said

"Don't worry, you'll be OK".

I don't know about OK, but I was getting better enough to move my legs and arms. That is leg and arms, pointing to my itchy leg, the white suits coldly stated

"Oh, that was amputated months ago, you'll be fine".

At this point, all I could give those hacks was a fist and a finger.

"Oh, sir, no need to carry on that way". The head white suit said

"We have good news for you Sir. Today your feeding tubes will be coming out and shortly after you'll be able to talk".

The Enemy Within

What could I say? What could I do? When Kelly Ling arrived, all I could write on my sketch pad was Lynch? Davidson? Leg? She explained that Lynch and Davidson were already dead men, because the cancer as too far advanced. They stayed in Nam to help others like us and the United States paid their families well. They knew they were goners and didn't want their friends and families to see the cancer eat them up. As she told me this gut-wrenching news, tears rolled down our faces.

The Government paid all of us off with hush money and we went home to our new home to live out our remaining years. Kelly Ling was also very sick with cancer. Soon enough, the white suits said we have no choice but to come "in" and live at Walter Reed Hospital. We knew we were to be their test subjects.

Joe and Kelly Ling had enough of the lie, but couldn't get enough of each other. Sitting in the car in the garage, Joe held Kelly Ling as the motor ran.

"You know Joe, the good die young".

"If that's so Honey, we'll live forever".

"Joe, do you think the carbon monoxide will ruin their test"?

 "I hope so Kelli Ling".

The hose connected to the exhaust went to the closed window, as Joe and Kelly Ling slept forever.

- THE END -

AUTHOR: JOSEPH WILLIAMS

www.ingramcontent.com/pod-product-compliance
Lightning Source LLC
Chambersburg PA
CBHW071343130626
46556CB00005B/2006